"Mary...darling...can you hear me?"

Mary moaned. "Make it go away," she muttered.

Daniel frowned. "Make what go away?"

"The dreams. Make them all go away."

He shook his head slightly, ignoring her rambling remarks as he continued to dab her forehead with a dampened handkerchief. Before Daniel could answer her, Hope slid between them.

"Daddy, what's the matter with Mommy?"

"I think maybe she got too hot."

Mary found herself focusing on the sound of their voices and wondered, when she looked, which dream she would be in—the one from her past or the one from the future. The urge to scream was uppermost in her mind as she slipped in and out of her fantasy.

Curious as to what she'd see next, she opened her eyes....

Dear Reader,

It's always cause for celebration when Sharon Sala writes a new book, so prepare to cheer for *The Way to Yesterday*. How many times have you wished for a chance to go back in time and get a second chance at something? Heroine Mary O'Rourke gets that chance, and you'll find yourself caught up in her story as she tries to make things right with the only man she'll ever love.

ROMANCING THE CROWN continues with Lyn Stone's *A Royal Murder*. The suspense—and passion—never flag in this exciting continuity series. Catherine Mann has only just begun her Intimate Moments career, but already she's created a page-turning military miniseries in WINGMEN WARRIORS. *Grayson's Surrender* is the first of three "don't miss" books. Look for the next, *Taking Cover*, in November.

The rest of the month unites two talented veterans—Beverly Bird, with *All the Way*, and Shelley Cooper, with *Laura and the Lawman*—with exciting newcomer Cindy Dees, who debuts with *Behind Enemy Lines*. Enjoy them all—and join us again next month, when we once again bring you an irresistible mix of excitement and romance in six new titles by the best authors in the business.

Leslie J. Wainger
Executive Senior Editor

Please address questions and book requests to:
Silhouette Reader Service
U.S.: 3010 Walden Ave., P.O. Box 1325, Buffalo, NY 14269
Canadian: P.O. Box 609, Fort Erie, Ont. L2A 5X3

The Way to Yesterday

SHARON SALA

Silhouette®

INTIMATE MOMENTS™

Published by Silhouette Books

America's Publisher of Contemporary Romance

SILHOUETTE BOOKS

ISBN 0-373-27241-3

THE WAY TO YESTERDAY

Copyright © 2002 by Sharon Sala

Visit Silhouette at www.eHarlequin.com

Printed in U.S.A.

Books by Sharon Sala

Silhouette Intimate Moments

Annie and the Outlaw #597
The Miracle Man #650
When You Call My Name #687
Shades of a Desperado #757
Ryder's Wife #817
Roman's Heart #859
Royal's Child #913
A Place To Call Home #973
Mission: Irresistible #1016
Familiar Stranger #1082
The Way to Yesterday #1171

*The Justice Way

Silhouette Books

36 Hours
For Her Eyes Only

3, 2, 1...Married!
"Miracle Bride"

Going to the Chapel
"It Happened One Night"

SHARON SALA

is a child of the country. As a farmer's daughter, her vivid imagination made solitude a thing to cherish. During her adult life, she learned to survive by taking things one day at a time. An inveterate dreamer, she yearned to share the stories her imagination created. For Sharon, her dreams have come true, and she claims one of her greatest joys is when her stories become tools for healing.

During my lifetime,
there have been many people who've
made promises to me. Some have been diligent
in keeping the pledges they made, while others
swiftly forgot or ignored the fact that they'd
once given their word.

I want to dedicate this book to three very special people
who have been forever faithful to me in this respect.

First, to my agent, Meredith Bernstein.
Thank you for your honesty and your constancy
and your belief in what I do.

Next, to my editor, Leslie Wainger.
Thank you for trusting me enough to let me
tell my stories my own way.

Last, but not least, to Dianne Moggy.
Thank you for taking me in at MIRA
and letting me stretch my wings and fly.

Three ladies who are, to me, the epitome of class.

Thank you for your presence in my life.

Chapter 1

"I'm sorry Ms. O'Rourke, but your friend had to cancel your luncheon appointment. She said to tell you that the school called. Her daughter is ill and she had to go home. She tried to reach you at your office but you'd already left. May I seat you at a table for one?"

Mary Faith O'Rourke shook her head. "No, thank you. I won't be staying," she said softly, and walked out of The Mimosa without looking back.

It wasn't as if she'd wanted to come. For the past six years she hadn't wanted to do anything but die, and today was no exception. Exactly six years ago today, her husband and child were killed in front of her eyes.

Her friends worried about her, and in the back of her mind, she appreciated their kindnesses and sincerity. But they simply did not understand. Oh, they knew what had happened, but they didn't know the details or the guilt with which Mary lived.

Yes, she had been standing in her front yard when her husband had backed out of the driveway with their baby in the car. And yes, she had heard, before she'd seen, the police car come careening around the corner in pursuit of another vehicle. And yes, she had yelled at Daniel—screaming for him to stop. But they didn't know that the reason he'd been leaving the house was because they'd had a fight, or that the last words they'd spoken to each other had been in anger. They would never understand how insidious guilt was, or that she had tried so hard to die along with them when the three cars had collided and then burst into flames. Watching Daniel and their baby daughter die in that fire had destroyed her spirit. Now, she was just waiting for her body to catch up.

She glanced at her watch. It was a whole hour before she had to be back at work at the dress shop across town and since food was the farthest thought from her mind, she started to wander the streets.

It had been years since she'd been in this part of Savannah, but her friend had been insistent, raving about the renovations that had been done and the new businesses that had sprung up afterward. Mary had to admit that the place looked good. Old cement had been removed from the sidewalks, revealing a herringbone pathway of ancient, red bricks. Trees lined the curbs on both sides of the street, laying down a wide swath of shade for the shoppers who were on foot. Dainty trellises covered with climbing ivy and bougainvillea partially hid the tiny alleys between the buildings, giving the area an old-world appearance.

Mary walked and looked, but without really seeing. As she stopped at a crosswalk, waiting for the light, she overheard the conversation between the two women in front of her. Three children had gone missing from Savannah schools over the past six weeks, the latest only the day before yesterday. With no clues as to what had happened to them, Mary could only imagine the parents' fears. She knew the meaning of loss and of mind-numbing fear, and she felt guilt that she had prayed for the children's safe return without actually believing it would happen. The truth was, Mary had lost her faith in God and humanity.

She continued to walk, absently window-shopping without interest in buying. It wasn't until later when she stopped in front of a jewelry store to look at the window display that she realized she was lost. Curious, rather than concerned, she turned around, intent on searching for familiar landmarks, when the store across the street caught her attention.

The name over the doorway intrigued her. Time After Time. But when she realized it was an antique shop, pain hit her with the force of a fist to the gut, leaving her weak and motionless.

Before she and Daniel had married, antiquing had been one of their favorite pastimes. She loved old cookbooks and tiny treasures that were often overlooked by the true collectors. But that was back when they had still been happy, when his family hadn't known she existed. She shuddered. God. How many times in the past six years had she relived those last moments of their lives? Remembering the fights was like being stabbed repeatedly in the heart, and always because of the same thing.

His parents hated her, and she hadn't known how

to make him understand. She couldn't forget the sounds of her baby's shrieks, echoing above their own shouts, and feeling the guilt of knowing that she was frightened by their anger and harsh words.

She had known Daniel was frustrated with everything, including her constant tears and her inability to get along with his family. She had lived in fear that he would get fed up with her and leave, then knowing if that happened that her world would come to an end. And it had happened, but not as she'd expected. She had feared that he would leave her, but not that he would die in the process.

A car sped past in front of her, shattering her concentration.

God...how much longer do I pay penance before you put me out of my misery?

As usual, she got no answer to the question. Weary all the way to her soul, she started to turn away, barely missing a young boy on a bicycle as he came flying around a corner. In reflex, she jumped off the curb to keep from being hit and when she turned around, realized she was halfway across the street on her way to the antique store.

Longing for a connection with the man that she'd loved and lost, she started toward the store, hesitating only briefly as she reached the door. When she stepped inside, she paused and took a deep breath. The scent of well-oiled wood and ancient books mingled with the faint layer of dust on the jumbled up counter. To a true antique buff, it was like waving free money in front of an addicted gambler.

Telling herself she was a glutton for punishment, she let the door shut behind her. As it did, a small bell jingled from somewhere overhead. At the same moment, her gaze caught and held on the old man behind the counter.

She hadn't seen him at first, but when the bell sounded, he'd looked up and the movement had caught her eye. He was tiny and stooped and looked as old as the jumble of artifacts in the store. He had a tube of glue in one hand and a pair of tweezers in the other. She could just see the corner of a picture frame on the table in front of him and supposed he was trying to repair something that had broken.

"I'm just looking," she said.

He nodded and then returned to his task.

A slight shift of relief moved through her when she realized he wasn't going to follow her around in the store, trying for the hard-sell approach. She and Daniel had always liked to browse on their own.

Her nose wrinkled slightly in reaction to the musty odors as she moved toward the back of the store. The farther back she went, the more narrow the aisle became. Finally, she found herself holding the skirt of her dress against her body to keep from sweeping the dust off from an assortment of old tables and chairs.

Despite her initial nervousness in coming inside, she quickly lost herself in what Daniel used to call her "search mode." She shopped from instinct rather than a skill of knowing true antiques, and her purchases had always reflected that. She bought because she liked a piece, rather than due to any value it might have. In all those precious years with Daniel, her favorite purchase was still a small fluted vase for which she'd paid the huge sum of fifty cents. It was barely big enough to hold a single sprig of honeysuckle, but its fragility reminded her of a kinder, gentler time and place. If she closed her eyes, she could still see the laughter on his face when she'd crowed with delight at the find.

Determined to proceed, she jutted her chin and pushed past the dusty jumble toward a single counter at the back of the room.

There, in the middle of the mess, was a small glass case filled with an assortment of jewelry. The padlock on the case was rusty, which went rather well with the thick layer of dust on top of the glass. Determined to look inside, she took out a tissue and gave the dust a quick swipe. The moment she did, she knew she wanted to see more.

She turned and called out to the old man up front.

"Sir...I'd like to see the jewelry inside this case. Do you have the key?"

She heard the sound of chair legs scooting against wood and then the squeak of a drawer opening and closing. A few seconds later, the old fellow emerged and started toward her.

Mary tried not to stare, but there was something so compelling about his face that she couldn't look away. It was a mixture of age and grief and a knowing that comes with having outlived too many friends and family.

He stepped past her without speaking, removed the tiny padlock with surprising ease, then opened the case. For a moment, their gazes met and Mary felt as if someone had caressed her face. But then he blinked and the notion passed.

"Thank you," she said. "I'm interested in those rings. Do you mind if—?"

He walked away without bothering to comment and Mary shrugged. It was obvious from the dusty contents of the store that he didn't sell much, and if his behavior with her was normal, it was a wonder someone hadn't stolen him blind.

She dug into the display, soon realizing that most of it was junk, although the rings were another matter. Eagerly, she glanced through the lot, fingering them gently and sorting through the array, trying on one, then another. A few minutes later, convinced she'd seen all there was to see, she started to close the case when she noticed a tattered piece of lace stuffed in the corner of the case. Curious, she picked it up, then gasped in delight when a single ring tumbled out in her hand.

The band was silver, etched with an elaborate series of engravings that were reminiscent of a twining ivy and set with a single, clear blue stone. Blue topaz, she thought, and turned it toward the weak, yellow glow from the single bulb hanging from the ceiling. The light caught and held in the stone like an ember coming to life. She turned it in her hand, admiring the workmanship and wondering what it cost when she realized there was an inscription within. She squinted, trying to read the elaborate script and only with some effort finally discerned what was there.

I promise you forever.

Her eyes filled with tears. There was no forever.

Thinking of the man who'd first given this ring to his love, she clutched it in her fist and then closed her eyes. Daniel's face slid through her mind and without hesitation, she slipped the ring on her finger.

Just because it was there.

Just because the promise was forever.

Within seconds, her finger began to burn. She jerked back in shock and yanked at the ring, trying to pull it off but it wouldn't come. She cried out, both in fear and in pain. As she did, the little old man suddenly appeared before her.

"Oh my God...oh my God...Sir, please help me. I can't get this—"

He smiled and the pain disappeared. Again she felt as if someone had just kissed the side of her face. She held up her hand, but the old man just nodded, as if in understanding. Although his lips never moved, Mary thought she heard him tell her it would be all right. Before she could argue, a sudden wave of dizziness sent her reaching for a dusty old highboy to steady herself.

"I don't feel so good," she muttered, and knew she should have eaten lunch after all.

A faint shift in the air almost took her breath away, then the pressure in the room began to expand. Even though she knew she was standing still, it felt as if she'd started to turn. Around...and around...and around...the chairs and the tables, the dusty pictures on the wall began to move backward, like a carousel in reverse. Everything in the room began to turn, taking Mary with it. She wanted to close her eyes, but she was afraid if she did she'd fall off the world. The old man's image began to waver before her eyes, as if he'd suddenly lost substance. A sudden chill filled the air, and panic struck Mary dumb as the old man disappeared. She stared in disbelief at the place where he had been standing.

The scent of dust and camphor was thick around her as was another, less potent, but still definable scent: the scent of lavender and dried rose petals. She heard crying and laughing, then a single, thin high-pitched wail and knew it was her own. Something within her snapped and she felt herself falling.

When she came to, she was standing at her kitchen sink. The smell of baby formula was thick in her nose and she could hear her baby crying in the next room.

Oh God...not this. Not again.

Gritting her teeth, she felt herself turn, knowing that Daniel would be standing in the doorway as he'd been before—looking at her as if she was a stranger and not the woman he'd made a child with—not the woman he'd taken as his wife. She heard herself saying the same words and wanted to scream. She knew what she would say because she'd heard it every night for the past six years. Was this her punishment for still being alive when everyone she loved was dead? Was she doomed to replay her last moments with Daniel and Hope forever? Would this nightmare never stop?

"Isn't her bottle ready yet?" Daniel asked.

Mary turned toward the sink where the bottle was warming in a pan of hot water. She yanked it out, shook a few drops on her wrist to test for temperature and started past him when he stepped in her way.

"I'll do it," he said, and took the bottle out of her hands.

Mary felt his rejection as plainly as if he'd slapped her in the face. She turned and stared back at the room. The sink was full of dirty dishes, and there was a pile of laundry in the floor just inside the laundry room in need of washing. The scent of burned bacon from breakfast was still strong in the air, and she needed to mop the floor. In the next room, she heard the low rumble of Daniel's voice as he soothed their baby girl, then heard Hope's satisfied gurgle as she began feeding from her bottle. Her shoulders slumped. She was a failure. Everything she tried to do went wrong.

From their first date, she'd known he was the man she wanted to marry. His Irish charm had worked magic on her too-tender heart and their first kiss had turned her knees to jelly. She'd loved him without caution and gotten pregnant for her abandon. She had to admit that he'd never wavered when she'd told him she was carrying his child. He had seemed elated and had quickly asked her to marry him that very same night. But his family, which had kept her at arm's length from the start, was furious. As they were certain that she'd gotten pregnant just to trap their only child into marriage, their cool behavior toward her had changed to an underlying hate. And they were so good at it—never maligning her or making snide remarks when Daniel was in earshot, always waiting until she was on her own. The sheer force of their will was eating away at her sanity and causing friction between Daniel and her. He didn't understand, and she didn't know how to tell him without sounding like a tattle tale, so she kept her pain inside and let the infection of it spill out into their personal lives.

In the other room, Daniel looked down at his daughter's face, marveling at the perfection in such tiny features and felt his heart twist into a deep abiding ache. He'd had no idea that love such as this even existed. He had been certain that the love he felt for his Mary Faith was perfect and all-consuming and then he'd seen Hope being born. The bond had been instantaneous and he had expected their child to cement their love even more. To his surprise, Mary had begun to pull away—keeping her emotions to herself in a way he didn't understand. She rarely left the house and when she did, seemed to scuttle through the errands like a crab seeking shelter, relaxing only after they were home again.

As for his parents, she had completely withdrawn from them and he didn't understand why. It seemed the only time she was even slightly comfortable was when it was just the three of them, alone at home. She had to understand that his parents needed to be a part of Hope's life, too. After all, they were her grandparents. He knew that Mary had grown up without any family of her own, and would have thought she'd be elated to share his. But it was just the reverse. Daniel wanted to believe that her reluctance to be with his family was nothing more than needing to recover from giving birth. But Hope was three months old now and things weren't getting better. They were getting worse. He went to bed with a knot in his belly and woke up the same way. Without knowing why, he was losing his wife, and it scared the hell out of him. And because he was so afraid, his fear often came out in anger.

He heard Mary banging pots in the kitchen and sighed. He wasn't fooled. She did that to cover up the sound of her tears. He looked down at their baby, his heart full to breaking and felt like crying himself. They'd made this baby with so much love—where had it gone?

* * *

Mary squirted a dollop of dishwashing liquid into the sink, filled it with hot water and put the dishes in it to soak for a few minutes as she went to start the laundry. Her back ached. Her head throbbed. But it was her heart that hurt the most. Last night she had turned to Daniel in her sleep and awakened as he rolled over and shrugged out of her grasp. She knew it was only a matter of time before he told her he wanted a divorce. She couldn't really blame him. He didn't know what was going on between her and his family and she didn't know how to separate his love for her from his love for them. It was all a horrible mess.

She shoved a load of Hope's baby clothes into the washer, added laundry detergent and started the machine, then went back to the dishes in the sink. Without thinking, she plunged her hand in the water and at once, felt a sharp, piercing pain.

"Ooh!!" she cried, and yanked her hand back. It was dripping blood.

"Mary! What's wrong?" Daniel called.

"Nothing," she said, then grabbed a hand towel and quickly wrapped it around her slashed finger before dashing toward the bathroom.

Daniel looked up from feeding Hope in time to see Mary bolt through the living room and then down the hall. Hope was almost through with her feeding and already half-asleep. Concerned, he laid her down in her bassinet and then went to see what was going on. He walked into the bathroom just as Mary started pouring alcohol over the wound.

"My God!" he cried. "Honey…are you all right? What happened?"

"Obviously, I cut my hand," Mary snapped.

Her anger sideswiped him, leaving him frustrated and hurting. And because he hurt, he lashed back.

"I can't win with you, can I?" he muttered, yanked the alcohol bottle out of her hand and began ministering to her himself. "No matter what I say, it's wrong." Then he peered a bit closer, assessing the cut. "I don't think it needs stitches, but maybe we should go to the emergency room…just in case."

"We can't afford a trip to the emergency room," she said. "Just give me some Band-Aids. They'll do just fine."

Daniel froze.

Mary felt sick. Daniel looked as if she'd just slapped him. But if she went, Phyllis O'Rourke would find out and she would find a way to say something hateful about the money an emergency room visit would cost. She couldn't face another one of Phyllis O'Rourke's tirades. He didn't know that his mother had been sniping at Mary for weeks about the fact that her son was having to work too hard on his own and that she should be doing her part by going back to work, too. No matter how many times Mary had tried to explain that she and Daniel had made the decision together that she should stay home with their child, it never seemed to matter. Phyllis blamed Mary for everything wrong in Daniel's life.

Mary sighed. "Daniel…I'm—"

Hope started crying. Daniel took a deep breath and momentarily closed his eyes, as if trying to make himself calm. When he looked up, Mary actually flinched and took a step backward. That hurt him most of all. Dear God! Did she actually think he would strike her?

Hope's wails increased.

Suddenly, he snapped.

"Damn it all to hell, Mary Faith. That does it! I am taking you to the emergency room. We'll drop Hope off at Mom's on the way. No need exposing her to God knows what. And when we get home, we're going to talk. I don't know what's wrong with us...but I am sick and tired of being shut out of your life. Do you hear me?"

"No!" Mary cried, and clutched his arm. "Please don't take Hope to your mother's house. I don't need to go to the emergency room. It'll be fine. See...it's almost stopped bleeding."

Daniel ignored her and kept walking toward the living room to get their baby.

Mary followed, still begging him to stay, but her pleas fell on deaf ears. She watched in horror as Daniel got a fresh bottle from the fridge, packed the diaper bag and then picked up their crying baby. Almost instantly, Hope's crying stopped, but now Mary was in tears.

"I won't go!" she cried. "You can't make me."

Daniel turned, staring at her as if she were a stranger.

"Fine," he said. "Stay here. But I'm still taking Hope to Mom's and when I get back, we're going to talk."

He strode out of the house, put Hope in the baby seat in the back of their car and strapped her in, ignoring the fact that Mary had followed him out into the yard, still begging him to stay.

The moment he laid Hope down, she began to cry again. But Daniel couldn't let himself focus on her tears. Her diaper was dry and she wasn't in pain. She just liked to be rocked to sleep and he'd laid her down a bit too soon.

"Hush, baby girl," he said softly. "You're okay. You're okay. Grandma Phyllis will rock you back to sleep when we get to her house."

He closed the back door and then turned to get in when Mary grabbed at his arm.

"Daniel...please! Don't! You don't know what you're doing to me."

He frowned. "To you? Damn it, Mary Faith! Don't you know what you've done to me? To us?"

Panic began to rise.

Mary stepped back, watching in horror as Daniel got into the car and closed the door.

Her heart began to race—her stomach turned. She didn't want to be here again. She knew what was going to happen. She'd seen it every night in her sleep for the past six years.

Oh God...wake me up before the crash. Please...I don't have the strength to see it again.

Daniel started the car. Mary stood, frozen to the spot, listening to the sound of her daughter's shrieks. Daniel put the car in gear and began backing down the drive. Mary could already hear the sound of an approaching siren, but Daniel couldn't hear for the baby's cries.

Oh God...oh God.

The brown sports car suddenly appeared, careening around the corner and fishtailing as the driver tried to maintain control.

Oh God...oh God.

The police car came seconds later, sirens at full blast—lights flashing.

And Daniel is looking at me, not behind him.

Suddenly, Mary bolted, screaming as she ran, and threw herself on the hood of the car. Daniel hit the brakes and then put the car in Park just as Mary slid off the hood.

His heart was in his mouth as he bolted from the car. Dear God…if Mary had fallen beneath the wheels he would never forgive—

Suddenly, he became aware of the sirens and spun in shock, just in time to see the sports car spin out of control. A heartbeat later, the police car broadsided it and the cars exploded in a ball of flame.

Without thinking, he slammed the car door to keep flying debris from hitting Hope and threw himself over Mary's prone body.

Mary was in shock. The dream! It wasn't the same! It wasn't the same. Overwhelmed with relief, she started to cry. Thank God. Thank God. Maybe this meant she was starting to heal. Even if it was just a dream, she'd given herself a happy ending.

"Mary, darling…are you all right?"

Daniel's weight on her back felt wonderful, as did the sound of his voice in her ears.

"Yes, Daniel, I am now."

He pulled her to her feet and then held her tight, pressing her face against his chest as he stared at the two cars engulfed in flames.

"If you hadn't stopped me, we would have—"

"Don't say it," Mary begged, and put her hand to his lips. Then she moved from his arms to the car, opened the back door and lifted her screaming daughter from the seat. "It's all right, punkin…it's all right," Mary crooned. "Mommy's got you now. You're going to be just fine."

Daniel watched the two most important women in

his life walk back in the house, then got in his car and pulled it back up the drive, away from the flames. Already, he could hear more approaching sirens. The neighbors must have called the police. It was just as well. He'd been too shaken too think past his own family's safety.

With one last regretful glance at the cars and for the demise of both drivers, he hurried back into his home and found Mary in the rocker, singing softly to their daughter as she drifted off to sleep.

Without talking, he went into the kitchen, stood at the sink and stared down into the bloody water for a moment, then pulled the stopper. As the water began to drain away, he saw the knife at the bottom of the sink that had cut Mary's hand. Cursing softly, he laid it on the counter, refilled the sink with clean water and soap, and did the dishes. He could still hear Mary singing, but Hope was no longer crying. At least she was happy because now he felt like crying. He'd come so close to killing both himself and Hope.

Bracing himself against the top of the washing machine, he closed his eyes and dropped his head.

"Thank you, Lord," he muttered, then took the clean clothes out of the washer and dropped them into the dryer before grabbing the broom and sweeping the kitchen floor.

A short while later, he had finished with the morning chores. He went into the living room to check on Mary and found Hope asleep in the bassinet and Mary asleep on the sofa. Pain wrapped itself around his heart and squeezed. Not much, but just enough to remind him of what he'd almost lost. Then he picked Hope up from the bassinet and carried her into the nursery down the hall, covered her up with her favorite blanket and closed the door. She would sleep for at least an hour, maybe more.

He went back to the living room, gazed down at his wife's thin, pale face and then at the blood seeping from beneath the bandages on her finger and sighed. She probably needed stitches, but what was done, was done. He got a small towel and wrapped it around Mary's hand, then covered her with an afghan. She needed to sleep worse than she needed stitches, and he needed to think.

Chapter 2

Mary woke with a start, then sat up in fright. Hope's old bassinet was in the living room, her finger was throbbing, and it was almost noon. She wouldn't stop to let herself even wonder where that bassinet had come from or why her finger was wrapped up in a bandage and towel. The last thing she remembered was walking into an antique shop. How she'd gotten home was beyond her and why she was on the sofa instead of in her bedroom was beside the point. She had overslept and her boss at the dress shop was bound to fire her.

Thinking she would immediately call in to the store, she bolted to her feet, frantically searching for the phone, but it wasn't in its usual place. Then she saw the stroller by the front door and Daniel's jacket on the back of a chair and went weak with relief.

The dream.

She was still having the dream, and as long as she slept, Daniel and Hope were still alive.

She looked in the nursery. The baby wasn't there, but when she walked back in the hall and heard the soft rumble of Daniel's laughter and a high-pitched baby squeal, it made her smile. Following the sounds to the small patio beyond the kitchen, she found Daniel in a chaise lounge under their shade tree, holding Hope against his chest. She was on her back, her arms and legs beating the air as she gazed upward into the treetop.

She combed her fingers through Daniel's thick, dark hair, relishing the feel of it against her palm, and then leaned down and kissed the side of his cheek.

"You shouldn't have let me sleep so long."

He looked up and smiled. "Why not? You needed it, honey. Besides, where else would I rather be than with my girls?"

Mary conscience tugged. If only she believed that he meant it.

"Really, Daniel? Do you really mean that? In spite of…I mean, things haven't been…"

"Come sit by me."

She hesitated, then when he moved his feet to give her room, she sat. She glanced at Daniel and then focused her attention on Hope, laughing at the baby's antics, unaware that Daniel was watching her and not their child.

Except for being thinner and paler, and a little the worse for a constant lack of sleep, she was the same pretty woman she'd always been. Hair the color of caramel taffy framed a small, slender face. Sometimes he thought her eyes were blue. Sometimes they almost looked green. But he could always see the tenderness of her spirit looking out at him from within. Only now, Daniel was trying to understand where her uncertainty had come from. Before they'd married, he'd never seen her down or second-guessing herself. Now she seemed to do nothing else.

"Mary?"

She looked up and the expression on his face was a bit frightening.

"What?" she asked, and then caught herself holding her breath as she awaited his response.

"What's happening between us?"

Her shoulders slumped. "Nothing."

"It's not nothing," he said gently.

"You're right. It's me. I'm sorry. I don't know why I'm so mean and hateful." Her chin trembled. "I don't mean to be."

"You aren't mean or hateful," he said. "And it's not you. It's something else, isn't it?"

Tell him. Tell him how much Phyllis hates me.

"I don't know what you mean." She was saved from having to talk further as the phone began to ring. "I'll get it," she said, and ran for the back door, leaving Daniel with a heavy heart and unanswered questions.

A few moments later she peeked out the back door.

"It's Phyllis. She wants to talk to you."

Daniel looked at Mary. That sick, nervous expression was back on her face.

"Tell Mom I'll call her back later, okay?"

Mary nodded and then went back into the living room and picked up the receiver.

"Phyllis, he's outside with Hope. He said he'll call you later."

"You're lying. You didn't even tell him, did you?"

Mary's stomach knotted. "Of course I'm not lying. He said he'd call you back."

"I don't believe you," Phyllis snapped.

The phone went dead in Mary's ear. She replaced the receiver and then slumped where she sat. Leaning forward, she rested her elbows on her knees and covered her face, trying to regain her composure before she went back outside. But when she stood up and turned, Daniel was standing in the doorway.

Mary flinched, wondering how much of their conversation that he'd heard.

"I was just coming back out," she said, and made herself smile.

"Hope's wet," he said.

"I'll change her," Mary said, took her from Daniel's arms and escaped into the nursery.

Daniel's eyes narrowed thoughtfully as he watched her go. He hadn't heard the conversation, but he'd heard the panic in her voice. What the hell was going on? Better yet—why wouldn't she tell him?

He followed her into the nursery and slipped an arm around her shoulders as she fastened the last tab on Hope's diaper. Just for a moment, he felt her hesitate and then lean back against his chest, just as she'd done so many times before. His heart quickened. He couldn't remember the last time she'd let her guard down like that.

"Are you okay?"

The deep rumble of his voice, as well as the gentleness of his touch, was almost her undoing. She wanted to tell him now, in the quiet of their daughter's room, but then he took hold of the hand that she'd cut and placed a tender kiss in the palm of her hand.

"How about we give this poor little hand a rest? I'll make us some sandwiches for lunch and tonight we could order in. We'll have an early dinner...maybe watch a movie. It's been a long time since we've done anything for us."

She laid Hope in her crib and then turned, unaware that the shimmer in her eyes was a dead giveaway of her emotions.

"I'd love that. You choose the food. I'll choose the movie."

He grinned. "As long as you don't make me watch *You've Got Mail* again, you've got a deal."

Mary made a face. "But I like Meg Ryan and Tom Hanks."

"I do, too, but I've seen that movie enough already to last me a lifetime."

"Then how about *Sleepless in Seattle?*" she asked, fully aware that her two favorite actors also starred in that movie, as well.

He growled as he swung her off her feet.

"You pick the food. I'll pick the movie," he bargained.

"Chinese."

"*Lethal Weapon.*"

They laughed in unison and then walked out of the room arm in arm. For now, the tension between them had been shoved aside in the joy of the unexpected reunion.

Less than an hour later, the doorbell rang. Daniel was in the act of slicing tomatoes for their lunch.

"I'll get it," Mary said. The smile was still on her face as she opened the door, but when she saw the expression on Phyllis O'Rourke's face, it was all she could do to be civil. "Phyllis...what a nice surprise. Please, come in."

"Where's Daniel?"

"In the kitchen making sandwiches for our lunch. We'd love to have you join us."

Phyllis glared. "Isn't it enough that he works all week as a lawyer? Must he come home and feed himself, too?"

Mary's stomach began to knot. She held up her bandaged hand to add to a hasty explanation.

"I cut myself this morning. He's only help- ing—"

"It's always something with you, isn't it?" Phyllis said, and physically pushed Mary aside as she strode into the house.

Mary staggered, then steadied herself by grabbing onto the small table in the hall. Sick at heart, she turned around and saw Daniel standing in the door- way. The look on his face was somewhere between disbelief and fury.

"Mother?"

Phyllis turned, her expression full of indignation.

"I called you about an hour ago, did you know that?"

"Yes, Mary told me. Didn't she tell you that I would call you back when I had time?"

Phyllis looked as if she'd just been drop-kicked. She glanced at Mary and then back at her son.

"Well...yes...I suppose she mentioned it, but you didn't call and I needed..." She took a deep breath and started over, refusing to admit she'd been wrong. "Your Aunt Evelyn is in town. She and Hubert are coming to dinner tonight and I want you to come."

Daniel looked at his mother, then at Mary, who was still clutching the hall table as if it were a lifeline. Suddenly, things were beginning to make sense.

Mary braced herself, waiting for Daniel to accept and knowing that she would have to endure a night of misery when they went. But Daniel surprised her by refusing.

"Sorry, Mom," then he walked past Phyllis and put an arm around Mary and gave her a quick hug. "We've already made other plans."

Phyllis's lips went slack. If he'd slapped her, she wouldn't have been more surprised. She glared at Mary, convinced that the woman was, somehow, at the bottom of Daniel's refusal.

"But Evelyn hasn't seen your daughter and there's no telling when they'll be back in town."

Ignoring the whine in his mother's voice, he tightened his grip on Mary.

"Hope isn't just *my* daughter, Mother, she's *our* daughter, and I'm sorry we can't come. Tell Aunt Evelyn we'll send her some pictures, okay?"

Mary was in shock. She still couldn't believe what was happening or what had caused it, but it was all she could do not to giggle with relief.

"Want to stay and have lunch with us?" Daniel asked. "It's not much. I'm not as good a cook as

Mary, but she cut her hand pretty badly this morning and I'm filling in. I still think she should have gotten stitches, but she thought otherwise. Anyway, it's only canned soup and sandwiches, but I slice a pretty mean tomato.''

Phyllis wouldn't look at Mary and couldn't meet Daniel's gaze.

''No...I'd better not. Since I'm having company tonight, there are a dozen things I need to do.'' She smoothed a hand down the front of her dress and then lifted her chin and made herself smile. ''Thank you for the invitation, though. Maybe some other time.''

''Give our love to Hubert and Evelyn,'' Daniel said.

''Yes...yes, I will,'' Phyllis muttered. ''They're going to be disappointed.''

Daniel chuckled. ''Then maybe next time they'll call ahead and let people know they're coming.''

Phyllis didn't bother to comment as she let herself out of the house.

The moment she was gone, Daniel took Mary by the shoulders.

''Mary...''

She sighed, then looked up.

''Talk to me.''

''What is there to say?''

''You can start by telling me how long she's been treating you like this.''

Mary's chin trembled, but she wouldn't let herself cry.

''Since the day she found out I was pregnant and we were going to get married.''

"No way!"

"Oh, but yes."

"Why didn't you tell me?"

Suddenly, Mary's chin jutted mutinously. "And say what? That your mother thinks you would never have asked me to marry you if I hadn't gotten pregnant?"

"That would have been fine for starters," he muttered.

"I couldn't," she said, then pulled out of his grasp and turned away.

"Why the hell not?"

She answered, but the words were spoken so softly, he couldn't hear what she said.

"What did you say?"

She pivoted sharply, her voice rising in misplaced anger.

"Because I wasn't sure but what it might be the truth."

Daniel was momentarily speechless, unable to believe the words that had come out of her mouth.

"You can't be serious!"

She stood her ground without answering.

Daniel tried to draw a deep breath and choked on tears instead.

"My God, Mary Faith...how can you doubt me like that?"

Mary's lips trembled as her eyes welled.

"Oh, baby...don't," Daniel begged. "Please don't cry."

He pulled her close; his hands shaking as he tunneled his fingers through her hair, then rocked her where she stood.

"I promise you will never suffer another indignity from my family and I apologize for being blind to what they've been doing. Trust me. It won't happen again. I love you so much, sweetheart, and losing you would kill me."

"You can't lose me," she whispered. "And I love you, too, Daniel. Forever."

"Okay, then," he said softly, then gave her a kiss so tender that it stole her breath away.

"Are you real hungry?"

Mary tilted her head, meeting his gaze with a smile.

"Not for food."

"Thank God," he muttered, and swept her off her feet and into his arms. "Now if Hope will just stay asleep for a little while longer…"

Mary leaned her cheek against his shoulder as he carried her down the hall to their bedroom.

"It's been a long time," she said softly, as he laid her down on their bed.

"Too long," Daniel said softly, and began unbuttoning his shirt.

The last thought in Mary's head was a small prayer that this dream would not end.

It was three o'clock in the morning when the phone rang. Daniel jerked in his sleep and then reached for the receiver before he was fully awake, not wanting it to ring again for fear it would awaken Hope.

Mary sat straight up in bed, listening as Daniel answered.

"Hello? Mom! What's wrong? What? Slow down...slow down...you're not making any sense."

Phyllis took a deep breath and then started to cry.

"Oh, Daniel...it's gone. Everything is gone!"

"What's gone, Mom?"

"Our home. Our car. The clothes. All of my pictures."

Daniel swung his legs to the side of the bed.

"What are you saying?"

"The house caught on fire." She choked on a sob. "Everything is gone."

"Are you and Dad all right?"

"Yes, but—"

"Where are you?" he asked.

"Across the street at Bob and Julia's. Hang on a minute, will you? Your father is trying to tell me something."

"Yes, sure," he said, and wiped a shaky hand across his face as he began to visualize the enormity of the loss. It was the house he'd grown up in, and there was nothing left but memories.

Mary clutched Daniel's arm, her voice taut with anxiety. "What happened?"

"Mom and Dad's house burned down."

"Oh no! Are they all right?"

He nodded.

"Go get them. They belong with us."

Daniel sighed. Hearing Mary say what he'd already contemplated was a huge relief. After what he'd witnessed earlier, he'd feared the last thing Mary would stand for was having his parents under her roof.

"Thank you," he whispered, and then turned back to the phone. "Mom?"

"I'm here," she said. "Mike wanted me to tell you which motel we'll be at."

"No motel, Mom. We want you here. As soon as I get dressed, I'm coming after you and Dad."

Phyllis hesitated. She wasn't sure if she was ready to face her daughter-in-law under such intimate circumstances.

"Are you sure?" she finally asked. "I mean, your wife might not—"

"Her name is Mary, Mom, and it was her idea first. Not mine. I'll see you soon."

Phyllis heard him disconnect and then replaced the receiver. She knew Daniel. When he set his mind to something, there was no turning him back. She looked at her husband.

"Mike, go wash your face. Daniel is coming to get us."

Mary dashed into the spare bedroom as Daniel pulled out of the driveway. It would take him about twenty minutes to get across town to where his parents lived, then another twenty or so to get back. It would give her just enough time to put clean sheets on the spare bed and find some fresh clothing for Phyllis and Mike to put on. Her hands were shaking as she began her duties, trying to imagine the heartbreak of losing forty years of accumulated possessions and memorabilia.

Then suddenly she froze. She still had all the worldly possessions. It was her loved ones that were really gone.

In that moment, she felt herself trying to surface from the indulgence of this fantasy. Before it could happen, Hope let out a wail and Mary began resubmerging, pushing away the fear and returning to the dream—because it was safer—and because it was where she wanted to be.

She blinked, then looked up. The bedroom was still the same and Daniel's winter clothes were still hanging in the extra closet. With a sigh of relief, she pulled the last pillow slip onto the pillow and dropped it in place, making sure that the bed was turned back in an inviting manner, then bolted out of the room toward the nursery.

"Mommy's coming, honey. Don't cry."

She'd taken a coffee cake out of the freezer and had it thawing on the cabinet. Hope had been changed and fed and Mary was in the act of laying out a clean nightgown and pajamas when she heard Daniel's car in the driveway. With a last look at the bedroom to assure herself that everything was in place, she hurried to the front door. They were just coming up the steps as she opened the door to greet them.

"Phyllis...Mike...thank goodness you're both all right."

She took Phyllis by the hand and pulled her into the house. They were red-eyed and soot-stained and the smell of smoke was all about them.

"I'm so sorry," she said softly, then gave Phyllis a quick hug before moving on to Daniel's father. "Mike, tell me you're both okay?"

"As good as could be expected, I guess."

Mary nodded then her gaze moved to Daniel, as if seeking his approval.

"I've given your father a pair of your clean pajamas and you two can sort through other clothes later." Then she turned to Daniel's mother. "Phyllis, you'll find a clean nightgown at the foot of your bed beside Mike's pajamas. There are clean towels in the bathroom as well as shampoo and a hair dryer. Please use anything you need. When you've both had a chance to clean up, come to the kitchen. I've made some hot chocolate and there's coffee cake to go with it."

Mike O'Rourke seemed to go limp with relief, as if he'd been holding himself together by sheer will alone.

"Thank you, dear. We appreciate you and Daniel having us here and we'll try not to be a bother."

"Family is never a bother," Mary said.

Guilt rode hard on Phyllis's conscience as she let Mike lead her down the hall toward the guest room. She paused in the hallway and looked back. Daniel was standing in the shadows with his arms around his wife, holding on to her as if his life depended upon it—and she was holding him back—her head buried on his chest, her hands fisted in the fabric of his jacket. Quickly, she turned away, unwilling to admit that the fresh set of tears in her eyes were because of them, and not the loss of her home.

"Come on, Phyllis," Mike said. "You shower first."

She took a deep breath and lifted her chin as she walked into the room, quietly closing the door behind her.

Daniel gave Mary a swift kiss and then followed her into the kitchen. It was warm and comforting and smelled of chocolate and cinnamon. He took one look at the table set for four and hugged her again.

"You are a saint," he said quietly.

"No, Daniel. Just a woman fighting for a place in your world."

"You are my world, Mary Faith. You and Hope matter more to me than anyone or anything else."

She pulled back and looked at him then, her shy smile almost childlike.

"I know that...at least...I know that now. I'm sorry I doubted you."

"Forgiven," he muttered, and slanted a hard kiss across her mouth before he turned her loose. "Is there anything I can do to help?"

"I couldn't find the marshmallows for the hot chocolate. Do you know where they are?"

"Nope, but I can look."

"Thanks," she said, then fluttered nervously toward the cabinet. "I just want this to be nice for them."

He frowned. "I don't know that they actually deserve this, but I appreciate it, just the same."

She turned, her hands clutched against her middle.

"Daniel, please. Don't say anything to them about...well, you know. They've suffered a traumatic loss. Let bygones be bygones, all right?"

"Fine, but I'd better not hear one critical remark out of my mother's mouth or they'll be looking for that motel after all."

She smiled. "Thank you."

"Don't thank me yet," he muttered.

"The marshmallows, please?"

"Oh. Yeah. Right."

About a half hour later, Mike and Phyllis emerged from the bedroom, freshly showered and shampooed and wearing clean clothes. Daniel was waiting in the living room, watching Mary sleeping on the sofa. When he heard the door open, he arose, then pulled the afghan a little higher over her shoulder before he went to meet them.

"Where's Mary?" Mike asked.

Daniel pointed toward the sofa. "Asleep. She doesn't get much rest these days and Hope's already had her up once tonight. I thought it best to let her sleep."

Phyllis peered over the sofa and stared at the thin, pale face of the woman who'd married her son. Even from here, she could see dark circles of fatigue beneath her eyes and felt a quick spurt of remorse. She remembered how hard it had been to be a mother for the first time and how exhausted she'd been. Fortunately, she'd had her mother and older sister nearby who'd been of tremendous help and support. She looked at Mary again. Mary had no one.

As Daniel and Mike moved into the kitchen, she turned away and followed them, well aware that she had Mary to thank for her present safety and comfort.

"What's all this?" Phyllis asked, as she entered the kitchen.

Daniel took the pot of hot chocolate from the stove where Mary had been keeping it warm and began to pour it into their mugs.

"Cinnamon coffee cake, freshly warmed in the

oven, and hot chocolate,'' he said, as the warm, sweet scent filled the room. ''Mom, will you cut the cake?''

Reluctantly, Phyllis picked up the knife and thrust it through the cake. It parted tenderly beneath the blade in perfect slices.

''It looks wonderful,'' Mike said.

Daniel beamed. ''It tastes even better. Mary's a really good cook.''

Phyllis served up the slices, then sat down in her chair. The horror of what they'd just endured had been lessened by the warmth and comfort of this home. Up until she'd walked into the kitchen, she hadn't been able to get the smell of burning wood and smoke from her nostrils. Now all she could smell was hot chocolate and cinnamon. She was clean and safe and everything they'd lost could be replaced.

Then she looked at Daniel, watching the animation on his face as he talked to Mike about his plans for the future and knew there was one thing she'd almost lost that was irreplaceable—her relationship with their son.

''How's the cake, Mom?''

Phyllis blinked, then made herself smile and take a bite.

''Very good,'' she said, although the guilt she was feeling threatened to choke her. ''I wonder if this is from a mix.''

''Nope. It's out of one of her old cookbooks. She collects them, you know. One of her favorite things to do is to prowl antique stores for cookbooks, although she hasn't had a chance to do that for quite some time now. Hope is a pretty demanding little squirt.''

Mike chuckled. ''Then she takes after you, boy. I well remember how many nights you kept your mother and I up. You had your days and nights turned around for a good four months. I used to tease Phyllis about finding a way to return the merchandise.''

Daniel laughed. ''Yes, that's the thing about having a family. You'd better be darn ready to give up every indulgence you once enjoyed.''

''It's fine if you've had a hand in the decision to be a parent,'' Phyllis said.

The smile froze on Daniel's face.

''Mother, I'm going to chalk that up to the stress you were under tonight. But I better not ever hear you say another denigrating word to Mary or about her...do you understand?''

Phyllis paled. ''I didn't—''

''Yes, you did,'' Daniel said. ''And Mary didn't tell me. I heard you myself, remember?'' Then he looked at both of his parents and sighed. ''She didn't get pregnant...*we* did. And I couldn't have been happier. I have been in love with Mary almost from the first date. I'd already put a down payment on an engagement ring when she told me she was pregnant. It didn't change anything I'd planned except the date.''

Phyllis looked stunned. ''But you never said...I didn't know that—''

''Mom...I was twenty-six and long past telling you everything that went on in my life. The fact that I introduced you to Mary on our second date should have been warning enough that I was serious. How many other girls had I brought home before her?''

Phyllis frowned. ''None.''

''I rest my case.''

She looked at Mike and then sighed. ''And I apologize. I was wrong.''

''Fine…but I'm not the one who deserves the apology, am I?''

Phyllis stifled a groan. The last thing she wanted to do was face her daughter-in-law with this guilt. But she'd already lost a lot this night. She didn't want to lose what was left of her family as well.

''I'll tend to it tomorrow.''

Daniel gave her a cool look. ''And I hope with more meaning than you just implied.''

Phyllis had the good grace to blush.

Chapter 3

Mary woke up on the sofa with the first rays of morning sun shining in her eyes. The last thing she remembered was sitting beside Daniel and—

Oh lord! Mike and Phyllis were here!

She sat up with a jerk and then jumped to her feet. What must they think?

When she dashed into the kitchen and found it neat and gleaming, she groaned. Another mark against her. Phyllis would find a way to insinuate how Daniel had to do all the work. She pivoted quickly and started down the hall, expecting the doors to open and see accusing fingers pointed in her direction. Instead, she was met with the soft, but familiar, sounds of muted snores from the spare bedroom.

Thankful that her in-laws were still asleep, she peeked into her bedroom. Their bed was empty and she could hear the shower running. Daniel was up and getting ready for work. His diligence at the law office was starting to pay off and she knew he didn't want to give anyone an excuse to deny him a future partnership.

With a small sigh of relief, she moved across the hall to the nursery and pushed the door inward. Hope was lying on her back, waving her arms at the Mother Goose mobile hanging over her crib.

"Good morning, pretty girl," Mary whispered.

The baby turned toward the sound of her mother's voice and started to squeal.

Mary laughed as she picked Hope up and then laid her down on the changing table.

"A dry diaper and a warm bottle, in that order, little lady. How does that sound?"

Hope squinched her face into a tiny grimace and squeaked in disapproval when Mary began unsnapping the legs on her one-piece pajamas.

"Oh, it can't be all that bad," Mary crooned, as she deftly cleaned the baby and fastened a new diaper in place. "I'll hurry. I promise. Okay?"

A couple of snaps later and Hope was good to go. Mary picked her up, cradling her against her chest as she walked out the door, cherishing the feel of baby curls under her chin as well as the satin-smooth texture of Hope's delicate skin.

She met Daniel in the hall, and to her surprise, he was wearing sweats and a T-shirt, rather than his usual suit.

"Daniel, you're going to be late."

"I'm staying home today. I've already called in."

Mary felt a small surge of panic. "Is that okay?"

He knew her fear stemmed from more than worry about his job, but there was nothing much he could do other than what he'd already done.

"It's more than okay," he said. "They were very sympathetic to what happened to Mom and Dad. I had no pending court cases and the paralegal is still gathering research for that brief that's due next week, so my work will not suffer." Then he wrapped his arms around Mary and Hope and gave both of them a quick kiss. "Besides, I'd rather spend the day with my two best girls than go sift through the constant mess of our judicial system."

Mary nodded, but the frown on her face stayed in place as they walked toward the kitchen.

"You shouldn't have let me sleep last night. What must your parents have thought?"

"That you were exhausted and that you make damned good coffee cake."

She paused. "Really?"

He smiled and took Hope out of her arms. "Yes, really. Now go heat up Miss Thing's bottle. I'll feed her while you make us some coffee, okay?"

Mary's heart swelled with love as she handed the baby to Daniel. Their dark hair and stubborn chins were so identical it was almost comical.

"Okay, and I think I should start breakfast. Your parents probably have a lot to deal with today and won't want to be delayed."

"Honey…take it easy," he said. "My parents are still asleep and there are no deadlines to be met. Not in this house. Not today."

She smiled and nodded, then took a bottle out of the refrigerator and began heating it as Daniel sat down in the window seat. Bracing his long legs against the other side of the window frame, he laid the baby down in his lap. When she stretched and then began kicking him in the stomach, he laughed.

It occurred to him as he watched Mary busying herself at the sink that he was quite possibly the luckiest man alive. He thought back to yesterday—to all the turmoil that had been in their lives and how close he'd come to killing himself and Hope. If Mary hadn't thrown herself on the hood of the car, he wouldn't have stopped, and if he hadn't stopped, he would have backed right into the speeding driver and the police cruiser that was in pursuit. As it was, two men had died horrible deaths, and they'd been spared.

It was still difficult for him to accept that his mother had been so mean to Mary. What was even worse was that Mary had been afraid to tell him. He tickled the little roll of fat under Hope's baby chin and then looked up at his wife.

"Mary?"

The tremor in Daniel's voice made Mary turn abruptly, thinking something was wrong with Hope. But the baby was momentarily pacified by the sunlight coming through the trees outside the window.

"What?"

"I love you."

Emotion hit her like a fist to the gut.

"Oh, Daniel…I love you, too."

"You have nothing to worry about. Do you understand?"

Mary sighed, unaware that her shoulders slumped slightly in relief. But Daniel saw it and knew that his decision to stay home today as a buffer between his mother and his wife had been wise.

"Yes, I understand," Mary said, then lifted Hope's bottle out of the water and dried it off before testing a few drops on her wrist. "It's ready," she said, and brought it to him.

Daniel lifted his mouth for a kiss, which she happily supplied, then groaned softly when he refused to relinquish the connection.

She knew what he wanted and the thought of lying beneath his beautiful hard body made her ache. But with their unexpected houseguests just down the hall, what they both wanted was definitely not going to happen. Finally, it was Mary who pulled back.

"Daniel...we can't," she whispered. "Your parents..."

He frowned as he took the bottle and poked it into Hope's eager little mouth.

"I know. I know," he muttered. "But this won't be forever and when they're gone..."

She hugged the thought to herself as she turned back to the task at hand, which would be making breakfast.

"What sounds good this morning?" she asked.

"You," Daniel muttered. "But I'll settle for bacon and eggs."

She grinned and combed her fingers through his hair in a gentle, loving manner.

"And biscuits?"

He rolled his eyes in pretend passion. "Oh yeah." Then he added. "Better double the recipe. They're Dad's favorite, too."

"What about your mother?" she asked. "If she doesn't care for them I can make her some—"

He frowned at the nervousness once again in her voice.

"Mary Faith, you do not worry about what my mother likes or dislikes again, do you hear me?"

"Yes, but—"

"No buts, sweetheart. She will be thankful for whatever we serve and you will not suffer her disdain or criticisms again."

Mary was too moved to answer. Instead, she took a large bowl from the cabinet and began assembling the ingredients for the biscuits. By the time Mike and Phyllis were up, she was dishing up the scrambled eggs and taking the biscuits from the oven.

"Man, oh, man," Mike said, as he entered the kitchen. "A guy could get used to waking up to food like this."

Daniel eyed the slight shock in his mother's eyes and took no small amount of satisfaction in answering.

"I already have," Daniel said. "Mary is a super cook." Then he handed the baby to his mother. "Morning, Mom. Here, say hi to your granddaughter and see if you can get a burp out of her while I help Mary get the food to the table."

Phyllis was torn between jealousy and devotion. It had been years since she'd gone out of her way to fix breakfasts like this, and the comment Mike had made went straight to her conscience. But the smiles of delight on her granddaughter's face rechanneled her focus. She settled the baby on her shoulder and began patting her back as she took a seat at the breakfast table. As she sat, she watched and she listened, and not for the first time since their arrival, began to wonder if she could have been wrong.

"Mary."

Mary jumped at the sound of her mother-in-law's

voice, then turned abruptly, almost dropping the load of clean bath towels she was carrying.

"Yes?"

Phyllis sighed. The anxious expression in Mary's dark eyes was nobody's fault but her own. She reached for the towels.

"Let me help do that."

"No, please," Mary said. "It's just a load of laundry. I can do it."

Phyllis frowned. "I'm well aware that you're capable, girl, but it's your third load, and frankly, I haven't seen you sit down since breakfast. Besides that, isn't your hand still sore?"

Mary glanced down at the bandage on the finger she'd cut yesterday.

"Well, yes, but it's healing."

Phyllis took the clean laundry from Mary's arms.

"We'll fold them on your bed, okay?"

Reluctantly, Mary followed her into the bedroom. When Phyllis dumped the towels on the bed, Mary took a deep breath and moved to the opposite side. For a few minutes, they worked in silence. It wasn't until the last washcloth had been folded that Phyllis laid it aside and then sat.

"Mary, there's something I want to say to you."

Mary flinched. The last thing she wanted was another confrontation, but with Daniel and his father gone to the insurance agency, she was all alone. She gathered up the stack of clean towels and carried them into the bathroom, then put them away. When she turned around, Phyllis was standing there with the hand towels and washcloths.

"Thank you," Mary said, and put them into the linen cabinet beside the towels.

Phyllis nodded. "You're very neat," she said, eyeing the even rows of linens inside the cabinet.

"Thank you. I suppose it comes from living in foster homes."

"What do you mean?"

Mary shrugged. "Well, I never knew how long I would be allowed to stay, so always having my things neatly together made it simpler to pack when social services moved me."

Phyllis frowned. "You never knew your parents, did you?"

"I remember my mother," Mary said. "At least, I think I do. But I was so small when they took me away." Then she turned, looking Phyllis square in the face. "She didn't give me away, you know. She died of cancer."

Phyllis sighed. "You've had a difficult life, haven't you?"

"From your standpoint, I suppose so. But I never knew anything else." Then her expression softened. "But now I have Daniel and Hope. They…and you and Mike…are my family now." Then she took a deep breath, needing to get the rest of this said before she chickened out. "I know you and Mike wanted better for Daniel. But I love him. So much. And I would never do anything to hurt him or make trouble for him. He and Hope are my life."

Phyllis felt like a heel. "Yes, I can see that," she said. "I've not been fair to you and I'm sorry." Then she turned away and walked back into the bedroom.

Mary hurried after her. "It's okay," she said. "Really."

Phyllis turned. "No, dear, it's not okay. I've been

horrible to you, but given time, I will make it right. I hope you forgive me?"

Mary's eyes welled. "Oh, Phyllis, thank you," she cried, and impulsively threw her arms around her mother-in-law's neck.

Phyllis hesitated briefly, then returned the embrace.

"It's me who should be thanking you," she said softly. "You have a generous heart, my dear. Daniel and Hope are lucky to have you."

Lucky to have you...lucky to have you...lucky...

A car horn blared, followed by a burst of angry curses and then the squealing of tires on pavement.

Mary jerked.

Reality and fantasy were beginning to separate within her mind and all she could think was *not yet. Not yet.* But no matter how desperately she tried, she couldn't hold on to the dream. Her head was spinning, her legs weak at the knees.

"Daniel," she moaned.

But there was no answer, only the smell of old wood and dust. In that instant, she knew it was gone. She opened her eyes.

The antique shop. She was still standing in the antique shop and Mike and Phyllis O'Rourke hadn't spoken to her since the day of the funeral six years ago.

In that moment, what had been left of her spirit died, too. There was nothing in her life but an emptiness that all the jobs and all the busy work would never fill. The only people who'd ever loved her were dead and she wanted to be with them.

With a shuddering sob, she stared down at the ring

on her finger. The engraving—*I promise you for-ever*—was a joke. Hating herself and life in general, she tore it off and flung it back into the case. There was no such thing as forever.

"No more," she muttered. "I can't do this...I don't want to do this. Not anymore."

She turned, only to find the old man staring at her from the end of the counter.

"I don't want the ring. I put it back," she muttered, and pointed in the general direction of the case. "I have to go." But her feet wouldn't move. She seemed helpless beneath the compassion of his gaze. Her eyes filled with tears. "You don't understand. They're dead, you know. They're all dead but me."

Then her composure broke and she started to cry.

Love doesn't die.

Mary stared. Although she'd heard the words, his lips had not moved. When he started toward her, shuffling his tiny little feet on the dusty, planked floor, she wanted to run, but he was blocking her only exit.

"Don't," she muttered, although she didn't quite know why she said it.

He'd made no move to harm her and had yet to say a word. When he reached in his pocket, she caught herself holding her breath. But when he pulled out a neatly ironed linen handkerchief and laid it in her hands, she felt shame that she'd feared him.

"Oh God," she moaned, and bent her head.

At the same time, she felt a hand at the crown of her head and then the old man was stroking her hair, as he might have a child. Mary shuddered as she lifted the handkerchief to her face and wiped away tears. What had she been thinking, behaving this way in front of a stranger? When she looked up, he was gone. The only proof she had that he'd been there was the handkerchief she was holding.

"Lord," she muttered. "I probably embarrassed him horribly."

She laid the handkerchief aside and started to weave her way through the narrow aisle, anxious to be away from this place. She'd been crazy to come in here to begin with. All it had done was remind her of what she'd lost. She wouldn't let herself think about why the dream had been different this time, because it didn't really matter. Her reality was a living hell and *it* hadn't changed.

The front door was open and she headed for it like a moth to a flame.

Out.

She needed out.

Away from the memories.

Away from the pain.

She fixed her gaze on the rug of sunlight spreading across the threshold and told herself that if she didn't breathe until she passed it, all the pain would go away. It wasn't the first time she'd played such a mind game with herself, but she was brought up short from escaping when a curly-haired little girl burst into the building.

"Mommy! Mommy!"

The brutality of the moment stopped Mary short. In her mind, it was but another bit of proof as to how perfectly cruel life could be. If Hope hadn't died—

"Mommy! Where are you?" the little girl cried.

Mary swallowed past the knot of misery in her throat and stepped out of the shadows and into the light. No matter how much it would hurt her, the child was obviously lost and afraid. But the words never came out of her mouth. When the child saw her move, the frown on her face turned to joy.

"Mommy! Mommy! We're ready to go! Daddy's going to buy us all ice cream and I want banilla with starberry sprinkles."

Shock spread across Mary's face as she stared at the approaching child in disbelief. Then over the child's shoulder, she saw the sunlight on the floor suddenly shrink as a man appeared in the doorway. At first, she saw nothing but a big, dark silhouette, but then he spoke and the sound of his voice grabbed her heart.

"There you are," he chided, and took the little girl by the hand before she could go any farther.

Mary struggled to take a breath. *Damn you, God...you took my reasons for living and left me behind. Now you want my sanity, too?*

The man looked up at Mary and grinned.

"Hey, honey. Did you find anything you can't live without?"

Mary moaned and took a short step backward. *Why was this happening?* That had always been a running joke between herself and Daniel when they used to go antiquing, but this wasn't funny.

Then the man moved past the doorway and further into the store. When Mary saw his face she started to shake. Black hair, blue eyes and that square jaw with a slight dimple in his chin. *Daniel? Oh God...Daniel.*

"Mary...darling...are you all right? You look a little pale."

He reached for her, steadying her with a hand to the shoulder, then he cupped her face.

She looked up in horror. She could feel his fingers on her skin. This wasn't possible. She took a deep breath and closed her eyes. PTSD. That's what it was. Post-traumatic stress disorder, brought on by her foray into antiques. When she opened her eyes, he would be gone. All of this would be gone. But when she looked he was still there, leaning closer now, and she could feel his breath on her face.

"Daniel?"

He smiled. "Definitely not the Easter Bunny," he teased.

She fainted in his arms.

"Mary…darling…can you hear me?"

Mary moaned. "Make it go away," she muttered.

Daniel frowned. "Make what go away?"

"The dreams. Make them all go away."

He shook his head slightly, ignoring her rambling remarks as he continued to dab her forehead and cheeks with a dampened handkerchief. Before he could answer her, Hope slid between them and put a hand on her father's arm.

"Daddy, what's the matter with Mommy?"

"I think maybe she just got too hot."

His daughter's voice trembled slightly. "Is she going to die?"

"No, baby…oh no! Mommy's fine. See! She's waking up right now."

Mary found herself focusing on the sound of their voices and wondered when she looked, which dream she would be in—the one from her past or the one from the future. The urge to scream was uppermost in her mind, but what was happening was inevitable. She was losing her mind. It was the only explanation for the fact that she kept slipping in and out of a fantasy. She shouldn't be surprised that it was finally happening. She was having a nervous breakdown. End of story. Curious as to what she'd see next, she opened her eyes.

"See," Daniel said. "I told you she was okay." Then his voice deepened as he caressed the side of her face. "Sweetheart…how do you feel?"

"Crazy," she muttered. "How about you?"

He chuckled and then winked at Hope. "I think the worst is over. At least your mother's sense of humor is firmly in place."

"Help me up," Mary muttered.

Daniel stood, then put his hands beneath her arms and pulled her upright.

"Easy," he warned. "You might still be dizzy."

Mary swayed momentarily, then slowly gained her equilibrium.

"Okay?" he asked.

She took a deep breath and then nodded.

"Mommy?"

Mary's stomach knotted as she looked down at the little girl.

"I don't have to get banilla ice cream today," Hope said.

Mary frowned, then remembered something being said about vanilla ice cream with strawberry sprinkles.

"That's very sweet of you, but I'm all right."

"Oh goody," Hope cried. "Ice cream will make you feel better, too."

Daniel slid an arm around Mary's waist and turned her toward the door.

"Hope, can you carry Mommy's purse for her, please?"

"Yes. I always carry it when Mommy's arms are full of groceries," she said, then picked up the shoulder bag Mary had dropped and slung it across her shoulder.

Mary fought the urge to laugh, but she was afraid if she started, she wouldn't be able to stop. Maybe she should tell someone what was happening. Then she discarded the thought. After all, who would believe her?

As they started out the door, she paused and looked back, but the old man was nowhere in sight. That figured. She'd probably imagined him, too.

When the sunlight hit her face, she squinted and ducked her head against the glare. And because she did, she missed the fact that she was being led to a waiting car. When they paused, she looked up, her eyes widening at the big, white Cadillac Daniel was unlocking.

"I walked here," she muttered.

Daniel frowned and ran his hand through her hair.

"What are you doing?" Mary asked.

"I was checking for a bump. You're not making a lot of sense right now and might have a slight concussion. I thought I caught you before you hit the floor, but I could be wrong."

"I didn't hit my head," she said. "I just lost my mind."

Hope giggled. "Mommy's funny."

Mary let herself be seated in the car and then watched as Daniel put Hope in the back seat. Without thinking, Mary turned around, got up on her knees and buckled the little girl into her booster seat. It wasn't until she had turned around and was reaching for her own seat belt that she realized what she'd done. It had been so natural. Something she'd done without thinking. Something she'd done a thousand times before. She pulled the sun visor down and then looked at herself in the attached mirror. Ignoring her pallor, she stared, trying to find the madness in the woman looking back. But all she could see was a slight expression of shock.

Then her gaze slid past her own reflection to the child behind her as Daniel got into the car. He reached for Mary's hand and gave her fingers a slight squeeze.

"Honey...are you sure you're up for this ice cream stop?"

"I have no idea, but we'll soon find out."

"It's not that important," Daniel said. "Hope won't mind."

"But I will," Mary muttered. "In fact, I'd say we have to go. I can't wait to see what happens next."

Chapter 4

Daniel was more than a little distracted by Mary's behavior as he drove through the Savannah streets. Even though it had been overly warm inside the old store, it wasn't like her to faint. When he came to a main intersection and stopped at the red light, he reached across the seat and threaded his fingers through hers.

"How are you feeling?"

Her eyes widened as she stared down at his hand and then he heard her take a deep shaky breath.

"Mary Faith...what's wrong?"

Mary didn't know what to say. She was convinced that this was nothing more than an extension of her other fantasy. The dead do not come back to life, but she'd never had a dream this real. If she only had a choice, she would choose this insanity rather than go back to the loneliness and misery of her life. And therein lay her dilemma. If she voiced her fears, would it make all of this disappear? The fact that she could actually feel Daniel's hand on hers was an unbelievable facet to this dream. To lose it—and him—again, would break what was left of her heart.

She managed a smile and opted for safety.

"I'm fine," she said. "Stop worrying."

Daniel grinned. "Now that's asking the impossible and you know it. I always worry about my girls." His voice softened and lowered so that only Mary could hear. "You're my heart, Mary Faith. If you hurt, then so do I."

Mary's eyes welled with tears. Impulsively, she lifted his hand to her lips and kissed the palm before cupping it to her cheeks.

Daniel groaned softly, then glanced in the rearview mirror before winking at Mary.

"Your timing could be better here. I want to ravish you madly and we're in the middle of a busy intersection with way too much company."

The heat in his eyes made Mary's toes curl. Suddenly, she remembered the feel of Daniel's kisses and the pounding thrust of his body between her legs. She bit her lower lip and then looked away.

Crazy. That's what she was. Stark, raving mad.

"Mommy, are you sick?"

The quaver in Hope's voice was enough to get Mary's attention. She turned around quickly, making sure the child could see her smile.

"No, darling, I'm all right. I think I just got a little too hot, okay?"

Hope nodded, but her big eyes were still dark with worry.

Daniel glanced in the rearview mirror. Her panic

was obvious and catching. He knew just how she felt. When Mary had gone limp in his arms, his heart had almost stopped. She was the center of their world. He winked at Hope in the mirror and then asked.

"Are you still up for vanilla ice cream, honey, or are you going to try something different this time?"

The change of subject was exactly what Hope needed.

"I'm still having banilla," she announced. "But when we get to the ice cream store, can I have my ice cream in a cone instead of a cup?"

Hope's innocent question shifted Mary's focus into the everyday business of parenting so smoothly that she answered before she thought.

"May I, not can I," Mary said, as she turned to Hope, then somehow knew she'd said that very thing a dozen times before.

Hope sighed. "Oh yeah...I forgot. May I have a cone?"

Mary knew she was staring, but Hope's expression was so like Daniel's she couldn't look away. Was this what Hope would have looked like if she had lived, or was this just a wider crack into insanity?

"Mommy...may I?" Hope persisted.

Mary blinked, as if coming out of a trance.

"What? Oh...uh...yes, you can have the cone but we'll have them put a little marshmallow in the tip of the cone like before, okay? Then when the ice cream starts to melt, it won't leak."

"Yea!" Hope cried, and settled back in her seat as Daniel accelerated through the intersection.

Mary felt herself nodding as she turned around, but her heart was hammering in her chest. With a near-silent moan, she leaned back against the seat and closed her eyes.

Like before? Where in hell had that come from?

Almost an hour later, they were on their way home. Hope was asleep in the back seat of the car and the taste of praline and pecan ice cream was still on Mary's tongue as Daniel turned right.

"Where are we going now?"

Daniel frowned. "Home."

"But this isn't the way to our house."

Daniel's frown deepened. The confusion on her face was real. Once again, he knew he should have ignored her resistance to a checkup and taken her straight to the emergency room. Something wasn't right.

He pulled into the circle driveway and parked beneath the portico, then turned to face her.

"Honey, we've lived in this house for almost three years."

Mary's eyes widened as she stared at the brick two-story house and the tall white columns bracing the roof of the portico. Then she closed her eyes and took a deep breath before she was able to face him.

"Isn't that silly of me? For some reason I was thinking of our old house over on Lee Street."

Daniel leaned across the seat and felt her forehead, as if she might have a fever.

"I still think you need to see a doctor."

Panic shifted, then receded. "And I think we need to get Hope in bed," she said.

Before Daniel could argue, Mary was out of the car and opening the door to the back seat. Gently, she unbuckled Hope from her booster seat and took her in her arms.

"I'll carry her," Daniel said.

"No, you get the door," Mary said, certain there were no keys to this house in her purse.

Daniel sighed, then shook his head and quickly did as she asked.

The shaded rooms were cool, a welcome respite from the sweltering heat of afternoon. But Mary's relief was short-lived when she realized she had no idea where her daughter's room was supposed to be. She stared up at the circular staircase and wondered if she could bluff her way through, but the worry was taken out of her hands when Daniel took Hope from her arms.

"You're not carrying her up those stairs," he muttered. "In fact, you need to take a nap, yourself. Come on, honey. I'll unload the groceries and put them up. I want you to rest."

Mary followed Daniel up the stairs, not because she particularly wanted to sleep, but because she needed to see the layout of the house without making a complete fool of herself.

As she watched him laying Hope on the bed in her room, she couldn't help but wonder about this constant confusion. This was *her* dream. So why didn't she just know this stuff?

She backed out of Hope's room into the hall and then turned around, staring blankly at the series of closed doors. As she stood, certain things began to emerge. The door directly across from Hope's room was a bathroom, decorated in three shades of blue. She didn't know how she knew it, but she was positive she was right. When she opened the door and peeked in, her heart skipped a beat. Just as she'd thought it would be.

Quietly, she backed out and then walked a few feet down the hall to the first door on her left. This was the spare bedroom. She closed her eyes, picturing what was behind the door. Immediately, she focused on a pink and gold comforter on a four-poster bed. And she knew that, in the corner, there was a matching armoire she and Daniel had found on an excursion to Atlanta two years ago.

Taking a deep breath, she looked in. It was there, just as she'd envisioned. When she closed the door she was smiling.

Okay, I've been making this too hard. It's still my dream. It can be any way I want it to be.

Daniel was coming out of Hope's room as she turned around.

"Why aren't you in bed?" he asked.

"Because I was waiting for you to tuck me in, too."

Breath caught in the back of Daniel's throat. The invitation in her voice was impossible to miss. He caught her up in his arms and carried her across the hall, toed the door open with his shoe and then kicked it shut behind him.

Mary knew before she looked that there would be a king-size brass bed and that the room was decorated with the colors of autumn. When Daniel laid her down, she felt, before she saw, the handmade quilt on their bed. As the familiar softness cushioned her back, she kicked off her shoes and reached for Daniel. There was no way to know how long this fantasy would last, and she didn't want to waste a moment.

A hungry glint fired in Daniel's eyes as he sprawled across her. Tunneling his fingers through her hair, a low moan rose from his throat as he centered his mouth upon her lips.

In desperation, Mary clung to him. It had been so long. But before she could remove her clothes, Daniel drew back with a groan.

"Oooh, baby, hold that thought. I've got to get the groceries in out of the heat."

He rolled away from her and then got off the bed. Before she could think, he was out of the room and on his way down the stairs.

Mary turned over on her belly and buried her face in the pillow in mute frustration, then moments later, sat up in bed.

The furnishings in the room were almost opulent, but had a comfortable, lived-in look about them that almost seemed familiar. Her gaze fell on the closet and suddenly, she bounced off the bed and ran toward it. As her fingers curled around the doorknob, she caught herself holding her breath in nervous anticipation. Slowly, she pulled the door open then stepped inside and turned on the light.

Daniel's clothing was hanging on the right in a neat and orderly manner, from suits, to sport coats to casual slacks. Blue jeans were folded and stacked neatly on a built-in shelf as were an assortment of T-shirts. A row of shoes was on the floor beneath the clothing and a small rack of neckties hung from the back of the closet door. Just as she would have expected it to be.

When she looked to the left, all the air went out of her lungs in one breath, as if she'd been punched in the stomach. An entire wardrobe of women's dresses, blouses, skirts and slacks—and in her size—were hanging on the rack.

Okay…so I'm dreaming in detail and color…and with sensation. So what? I've already accepted the fact that I'm losing my mind.

She stepped out of the closet and then turned off the light. Immediately, her gaze moved to the door Daniel had left open. She walked into the hallway and then into the room where Hope was sleeping.

For whatever reason and for however long this fantasy would last, she not only had Daniel back, but she had her daughter, too. The bond she'd had with the baby seemed nothing but a distant memory as she stared down at the six-year-old girl in disbelief. The longer she looked, the tighter the ache grew within her chest. Quietly, she tiptoed to the side of the bed, smiling at the one-eared bunny tucked beneath Hope's chin, and pulled the covers back over the little girl's shoulders. Then, reluctant to lose the connection, she lifted a stray lock of hair away from Hope's face, then leaned down and brushed her forehead with a kiss and as she did, felt as if she'd done it countless times before. Her heart swelled as she watched the little girl's eyelids fluttering in sleep.

This is my baby.

She watched her for only a few moments, then, afraid her presence would wake Hope up, she went back to the bedroom she shared with Daniel. For a few moments, she stood in the doorway, staring at the room and the feelings it evoked. Finally, she took a deep breath and began taking off her clothes. Seconds later, she was in the bathroom and stepping beneath the warm water jetting from the showerhead. It could only be symbolic, but she had a sudden urge to wash away every remnant of her old, sad life.

* * *

Daniel's heart sank when he saw the empty bed, then he heard the shower running and smiled. With a quick glance over his shoulder to make sure the door to Hope's room was still closed, he shut the door to their bedroom and then turned the lock. Mary had strewn her clothes on the foot of the bed. He added his to the pile and then headed for the bath.

The water was warm on Mary's skin as she closed her eyes and turned her face to the jets, but when she heard the shower door open then close, her breath caught in the back of her throat. Suddenly, Daniel's hands were tracing the length of her back, then around, cupping her breasts and pulling her back against his body.

"I love you, Mary Faith."

Tears welled against Mary's eyelids. To hear these words and to feel her husband's touch after all this time was staggering. Why and how this was happening was no longer of concern to her. If this was madness, then so be it. God knew it was better than what she'd had.

She turned in his arms, her heart pounding, her body weak with longing. With a soft, desperate moan, she threw her arms around his neck, relishing the roughness in his kiss.

Reluctantly, Daniel stepped back and began touching her all over, as if to assure himself that she was truly okay.

"You scared me today," he said softly. "When you went limp in my arms, my heart almost stopped."

Mary didn't want to think or talk about anything that had to do with before. All she wanted was Daniel.

"Make love to me, Daniel. I need to feel you on me...in me...I've been so lost."

Daniel turned off the water and then pulled her out of the shower and into their bed, his need to be with her driving caution completely out of his mind.

Mary had a few brief moments of cognizance as Daniel laid her down and then took the phone off the hook. After that, there was nothing left in her head but a series of mind-numbing images.

The slight drip of a faucet in the other room.

The beads of water still on Daniel's hair and the shuttered look on his face as he beheld the woman beneath him.

The sound of her own heartbeat loud in her ears.

The flare of Daniel's nostrils as he slid inside her body.

The shattering of her thoughts when he began to move.

The curl of need deep in her belly.

The building heat.

And then ultimately, the blinding insanity of release.

They lay wrapped in each other's arms, their hearts still pounding, their muscles weak and lax. But the unity that Mary had remembered was still there— even stronger than before.

Daniel had his arms around his wife, and when he rolled onto his back, he took her with him. Now, Mary lay with her cheek against his chest, feeling the strong, even heartbeat beneath his ear and closed her eyes.

Heaven. Sweet heaven to know this again.

"Love you, Danny."

He couldn't remember the last time Mary Faith had called him Danny, but the sound of it on her lips made him smile.

"Ah, baby…I love you, too," he said softly and held her a little bit tighter.

She sighed with pleasure.

Somewhere within the next few minutes, Daniel felt her go limp and knew that she slept. Carefully, he slipped out from under her and covered her with a sheet. Aware that Hope's nap wouldn't last much longer, he hurried into the bathroom and cleaned up the mess that they'd made, then dressed. Pausing beside their bed to look at his sleeping wife, he felt a familiar tightening in his chest. For all these years, it was still the same feeling he'd had the first time he'd seen her. She was the anchor to his world.

As he watched, a slight frown creased the middle of her forehead. Impulsively, he leaned down and brushed a kiss across her lips and as he did, the frown disappeared.

"Yeah, baby…I know. That's what you do to me, too," he said softly, and then closed the door behind him as he left.

It wasn't until much later that he remembered what she'd said just before he'd taken her to bed—something about being lost. But it didn't make sense. There hadn't been a day in the almost seven years of their married life that he hadn't known where she was.

Mary woke with a start, her heart pounding, her body covered in a sweat of panic.

Alone. She was alone.

"No," she moaned, and bolted from the bed.

She didn't want to be awake. She wanted back in the dream.

Yanking on her clothes with shaking hands, she tore out of the room. It wasn't until she reached the head of the staircase that she realized she was still in the house from the dream.

She stood, her legs shaking, trying to still a racing heart as the sounds of childish laughter floated up the stairs.

Hope? Was that Hope?

Without caution, she bounded down the stairs, following the sounds of her daughter's laughter and then found both Hope and Daniel in the kitchen having cookies and milk.

The moment Daniel saw her, he got up from the chair and went to her.

"Hey…look who woke up," he said, and then nuzzled her neck, whispering a more intimate welcome that only she could hear. "Ooh, lady, you look like a woman who's been had."

Mary went limp with relief, clinging to his embrace and trying not to weep.

"I wonder why," she said, cherishing the hard, hungry kiss that he slanted across her lips. Then she stepped out of his arms and peeked around at the table. "Hey, you! Did you save me any cookies?"

Hope giggled and pointed to the neat pile of raisins on her plate.

"Only the raisins."

Mary stared at the plate. "You don't eat raisins?"

Hope rolled her eyes. "Mommy…we never eat the raisins, remember?"

Mary stumbled to the table and then slid into a chair beside her daughter. She knew her voice was

shaking, but there wasn't a damn thing she could do
to hide what she was feeling.

"Yes…I *do* remember. We always give them to
Daddy, don't we?"

Hope giggled. "Yes, and we pretend that—"

"…they are pills to grow hair on his chest," Mary
added.

Daniel gave a pretend growl, popped the handful
of raisins into his mouth, then thumped his chest with
both fists. Hope shrieked with laughter and Daniel
loped around the kitchen like a monkey on the run.

Mary watched the pair's antics without comment,
making sure that she was nodding and smiling in all
the right places, while she struggled to understand.
This was nothing like a dream. She distinctly smelled
oatmeal and raisins and the scent of fresh-brewed
coffee, and there was something else about the moment that she couldn't get past. The longer she sat,
the stronger her sense of déjá vu.

The vague scent of meatloaf was still in the air as
Mary hung up the dishtowel and then dried her
hands. At first, it had been awkward, delving into
cabinets in search of bowls and pans, looking for
spices, trying to find dishes with which to set the
table for a meal. But the longer she'd worked, the
more comfortable she'd become. By the time the
food was cooked and ready to serve, she was on a
roll. More than once during the meal, she felt a little
like she'd felt as a child playing house, pretending
that everything was real. But she'd never tasted pretend meatloaf as good as what had come out of the
oven, or felt as much joy from the dolls that would
join her for tea parties as she did with this man and

this child. She felt like Alice, who'd fallen down the rabbit hole. For some reason, up was down, and down was up, and the faster she ran, the later it got.

But confusion paled in comparison to the love on Daniel's face and the sound of her daughter's laughter. Even now, the faint sounds of their voices in the other room made her want to cry. She couldn't count the number of times she had dreamed of such an evening. Giving the kitchen a last, satisfied glance, she decided that beggars should not be choosers and moved toward the other room where her family waited.

"Mommy!" Hope cried, and bounced up from the sofa where she'd been sitting to launch herself at Mary's legs. "I want to watch *101 Dalmatians...* please, please!"

Mary braced herself for the impact and then laughed when Hope's arms wrapped around her knees.

"You're going to be watching Mommy fall if you don't turn me loose," she said.

Hope giggled, then started dancing around in a little circle, still pleading her case.

Mary's first instinct was to never say no to the child that she'd lost, then looked to Daniel for support.

"Hey, kiddo," Daniel said. "Tomorrow is a school day. You need to get a bath and get in bed. You know the rules."

Hope's lower lip jutted, but she didn't argue.

Mary knew that a crisis had been averted and breathed a small sigh of relief.

"Come on, honey...you can use some of my bubble bath," she said, and then took a deep, shaky breath as an image flashed through her mind. Her—in the boutique section of Savannah Square—buying freesia-scented bubble bath and body powder. *God...how did this keep happening?*

"Yea!" Hope squealed, and headed for the stairs.

Daniel stood, then circled the sofa and took Mary in his arms.

"You sure you're up to this?" he asked. "You insisted on making dinner and doing the dishes, even after what you went through this afternoon."

Mary leaned against him, remembering the power of their lovemaking and suddenly shivered.

"Cold?" he asked.

She made herself smile. "No...just an unexpected case of goose bumps."

Daniel scooped her up in his arms and buried his nose beneath the nape of her neck.

"You like goose bumps? I can give you goose bumps."

She clung to him, thrusting her fingers through his hair and offering her mouth to his kiss. Again, the touch of flesh to flesh was like lightning—shocking and heated.

"Those will do for starters," Mary whispered. "I'd better hurry or Hope will have dumped the whole bottle of bubbles into the tub like last time."

Daniel rolled his eyes and then grinned. "Yeah...I remember. I smelled like flowers for a whole damned week."

"No, you didn't," Mary said. "It was only more like two days." The hair on the back of her neck suddenly rose. The line between reality and fantasy was blurring more with every passing hour.

"I stand corrected," he said, and then razed her

mouth with one last kiss as he cupped her backside and pulled her hard against the juncture of his thighs. "Feel that?"

Mary closed her eyes, giving herself up to the pure animal attraction between them.

Reluctantly, Daniel finally turned her loose, then lifted a stray lock of her hair from the corner of her eyes.

"You sure you don't want me to help Hope with her bath?"

"I'm sure," Mary said.

"Okay...but later, you have to help me with mine."

She laughed. "We've already done that once today."

Daniel smirked. "Cleanliness is next to godliness, Mary Faith. Would you have me become a heathen?"

"You already are," she said, and then headed up the stairs to find her daughter.

Chapter 5

It was twenty minutes after three in the morning and Mary had yet to fall asleep. Her eyes were burning with fatigue, her body trembling from the strain of trying to stay awake. Daniel's arm was across her shoulders, holding her firmly in place against the curve of his body. It would have been so easy to just close her eyes and let go, but the fear of losing what she had was too strong. This had become her reality. Going back to the emptiness of her other life would kill her, and that's what she feared would happen if she let herself sleep in this one.

Daniel shifted where he lay and then sighed. She felt his breath against her cheek and clung to him in desperation. Moments passed. Moments in which she remembered the scent of her freesia bubble bath emanating from Hope's skin as she helped her into her nightgown, and the heartbreaking sweetness of her daughter's good-night kiss on her cheek.

Mary stifled a sob as another thought surfaced. What if she had nothing to fear? Maybe she was already dead. Maybe this was heaven. If so, then there was no danger in going to sleep.

Yes! That must be it! Back there in the antique store when she'd started to get dizzy, she must have been dying! The fact that Daniel and Hope had been there to greet her should have been her first hint, because she'd never had dreams like that before.

Suddenly, the urge to look at this world anew drove away her exhaustion. She'd been looking at all of this wrong. It wasn't exactly what she'd thought heaven would be like, but who was she to quibble? With the people she loved best, it was perfect.

Careful not to awaken Daniel, she slipped out of his grasp and tiptoed from the room, anxious to see Hope again.

She was there in her bed, sleeping soundly, with that same old one-eared rabbit clutched tight beneath her chin. The urge to take Hope in her arms and never let her go was overwhelming. Instead, Mary straightened her covers and forced herself to walk away.

She paused for a moment in the hall, thinking of going back to bed and lying in the comfort of Daniel's arms. But the relief she was feeling wouldn't let her sleep. Not yet. Not now. She needed to see the house again, without the fear and confusion she'd had before.

Her steps were light as she moved down the staircase, her gaze curious and accepting as she studied the shadows made by the nightlight at the foot of the stairs. The carpeted floors in the living room were soft beneath her feet. The scent of bougainvillea was faint, but familiar. She turned toward the hall table and saw the vase of fresh flowers, then moved toward it, touching the clusters of tiny blooms with her fingertip, then bending to inhale the perfume.

A brass ship's clock on the mantel over the fireplace began chiming out the hour. The sudden noise within the silence of the room sent her spinning about. Sensing she was no longer alone, she looked up the stairs. Daniel was standing at the top, looking down at her in the darkness.

"Mary...are you all right?"

His presence was so real, so strong. There was no more doubt. She sighed, and as she did, gave up the last of her reservations. This now was her truth.

"Yes, darling, I'm fine."

"What are you doing down there in the dark?"

She hurried up the stairs and into his arms, relishing the comfort of his embrace.

"Oh...I just had a bad dream. I needed to make sure that everything was all right."

"Next time you wake me and let me be the one to chase away the ghosts. Okay?"

"Okay."

"Now that's settled, come back to bed. The alarm clock will go off before you know it."

Mary laughed softly to herself. Alarm clocks in heaven? Who would have known?

Hope downed the last of her milk and started to leave the table when Mary caught her and quickly wiped the milk mustache from her upper lip.

"Mommy...I've got to hurry," Hope wailed. "I don't want to be late for school."

No sooner had she said it than Daniel yelled from

the living room. "Hope! Come on. You're going to be late for school."

"Okay, okay," Mary said, giving the bow in Hope's hair a last fussing tug. "Don't forget your backpack."

"It's by the door," Hope said.

Mary followed her daughter's exit, unwilling to let go of the both of them at once. But Daniel was at the door with briefcase in hand and Hope was already shouldering her backpack when Mary got there.

"Don't forget I have dance class after school," Hope said.

A wave of panic hit swiftly, leaving Mary floundering for answers to questions she didn't know how to ask.

"Dance class?"

Hope rolled her eyes. "Mommy. I have class *every* Wednesday. Mrs. Barnes will bring me home."

"What time?" Mary asked. "What time will she bring you home?"

Daniel grinned and tweaked Mary's nose. "Five o'clock, honey. Just like always."

"Oh yes…at five. I was thinking of something else. Sorry."

Moments later they were in the car and driving away. Mary held her breath until they were safely out of the driveway, then stepped back inside the house and closed the door. It was just after eight. She started to smile. It was a long time until five o'clock. She would have plenty of time to prowl through the house and familiarize herself with everything in it. The daily paper was lying on the hall table where Daniel had laid it. She picked it up and carried it back into the living room, then tossed it on the coffee table to be read later. Her step was light, but her heart was lighter as she went upstairs because her family was, once again, intact.

Daniel pulled up in front of the school as Hope began scrambling with her backpack.

"Have a good day, honey," he said, and hugged her tight when she leaned over for her goodbye kiss.

"You, too, Daddy. I'll see you this evening, okay?"

"Yep. And don't forget Mrs. Barnes is picking you up after school."

"I know," she said, slamming the door behind her as she hurried up the front walk toward the building.

Daniel watched until he saw her enter the building with several of her friends, then he drove away. His mind was already shifting gears toward the preliminary hearing for one of his clients. He was well prepared and wasn't worried about that outcome, but he was concerned about Mary Faith. Even though she swore she felt fine and had shown no other symptoms of being ill, he couldn't get over how startled he'd been when she'd fainted in his arms. Her confusion afterward had cemented his worries even more. He made a mental note that as soon as he got to the office, he was going to give their family doctor a call. He wanted to hear someone else tell him there was nothing for which he needed to be concerned.

Howard Lee Martin stepped out from beneath the trees on the south side of the playground, watching as the last of the children entered the school building to begin morning classes, then jammed his hands in his pockets and started walking toward home. His mind was racing, his heart pounding with anticipation. He'd seen her again. A perfect little angel. As he walked, he began making a mental list of all the things he needed to purchase before the adoption. Not for the first time, he wished he'd gotten a chance to talk to her. He didn't know what kind of ice cream she liked best and he needed to know her favorite color. They would play dress-up. Little angels like her always liked to play dress-up. And then they would play house. Just the thought made him smile. His mother had let him make a fort under the dining room table when he was small, but little girls liked to play house, not cowboys and Indians.

As he pictured his mother, he grew sad. She'd been gone almost two years now. He thought of the two little girls he'd recently adopted and sighed. His children would never know their grandmother and that was too bad. She'd always wanted him to marry and settle down.

After she died, he'd tried to make friends, but he didn't know how. He'd joined a church, but hadn't been able to bring himself to approach any of the single women who attended. He'd begun hanging out at bowling alleys and coffee shops, watching the interplay between other couples and trying to figure out how it was done. Not for the first time, he thought that his mother had demanded too much of his time. He'd never had the chance to socialize with the opposite sex. It was only at his job that he'd come in contact with them, and then he'd been too shy to do more than speak.

Lately, his shyness had given way to frustration, then frustration to anger. It wasn't fair. Everyone had someone but him. That's when he'd decided to make his own family. Lots of single people adopted children. He read about it all the time. But the process hadn't been as simple as he'd believed. He didn't make enough money. He didn't have enough education. The excuses were endless, but they all boiled down to one thing. The authorities were not going to let him adopt. So he'd taken things into his own hands and done what he had to do.

A cat dashed across the street in front of him, just ahead of a small, black dog who was in pursuit. He laughed aloud, wishing the girls had been with him. They would have enjoyed the sight. It was important for children to interact with a parent, and he looked forward to the day when the transition from their old life to the new one was complete. Right now they were shy of him, but he had to believe the day would come when they would welcome him with open arms.

He glanced at his watch, making note of the time and hastening his steps. He had a lot to do before school let out today and he didn't want to be late. It was important to make contact several times before the day of the adoption. Children were taught not to talk to strangers, but after a few innocent meetings, his little angel would no longer view him as such.

Mary was digging through the back of her closet when the phone began to ring. Dropping the shoes she was holding, she backed out of the closet and answered the call with a breathless hello.

"Mary...are you all right? You sound like you're out of breath."

"Daniel... Hi honey! I'm fine...just made a dash for the phone."

There was a note of censure in his voice. "You're supposed to be taking it easy today but something tells me you're not."

"I haven't done one worthwhile thing this morning," she said. "I swear." His soft chuckle tickled her ear.

"Then how about meeting me for lunch?"

"Really? I thought you had court."

"Had it...still having it, but we're not due back for a couple of hours."

"What did you have in mind?" Mary asked.

"We don't have time for what's on my mind, but I'll settle for looking at your pretty face over shrimp scampi."

Mary laughed. "Just tell me where to meet you. We'll worry about the other stuff tonight."

"It's a deal," Daniel said. "You know that little Italian place a couple of blocks down from the courthouse?"

She didn't, but wasn't going to tell him that. "Yes, just give me enough time to call a cab."

"Cab? What's wrong with your car?"

Mary frowned. Another roadblock she hadn't anticipated. She hadn't owned a car since the day she'd seen theirs go up in smoke.

"Uh...I—"

"Don't tell me you've lost your keys again," he teased. "There's an extra set in the top drawer of the dresser. Just drive carefully, okay?"

"Uh...yes...okay."

"I'll get a table. Look for me inside."

"I will."

"Love you, honey."

Mary shivered as his voice softened.

"I love you, too. See you soon," she said, and hung up the phone.

She picked up her purse, then stared at it a moment before moving toward the bed. Impulsively, she turned it upside down and dumped the contents out onto the bed. Even though she saw the ring of keys falling onto the bedspread, it felt strange to accept the fact that they were there. Her hands were shaking as she picked them up. If this was the heaven she'd been given, then she should want for nothing. Okay. So she had a car. So what? She also had a husband and a daughter that she hadn't had two days before. Anxious now to get to Daniel, she stuffed the articles back in her bag and then hurried into the bathroom to put on some makeup and give her hair a quick brushing. A few moments later she was on her way out the front door.

The unattached garage was about twenty-five yards to the right of the house and she headed toward it at a trot. When she walked inside and saw the powder blue Jaguar in the south stall, she couldn't help but stare in disbelief. She'd never heard a preacher talk about a heaven like this, but she wasn't about to question another blessing. She jumped into the driver's seat, started the engine and backed out of the garage. Within seconds, she was out of the driveway and onto the street, heading downtown toward the courthouse. The sun was warm on her face and the wind tunneling through the partially opened window played havoc with the hair that she'd brushed, but she didn't care. How could anything as superficial as windblown hair matter when she had everything her heart desired?

Hope O'Rourke's little backpack was bumping against her shoulders as she marched out of the school toward the bus stops. Only Hope didn't ride a bus. She had to stand in line with the kids who were picked up by their parents and wait for the buses to leave. She craned her neck as she walked, looking for Mrs. Barnes's bright blue van, but she didn't see it. Her steps slowed as she sighed with disappointment. It wasn't the first time Mrs. Barnes had been late to pick her up and she hated having to wait. It always made her a little nervous, afraid that somehow she would be forgotten.

Her teacher was busy sorting through the waiting children, making sure they got on the proper buses, so Hope slipped out of line and dawdled toward one of the benches beneath the big shade trees by the street. She knew she was supposed to wait in line, but today she was tired and hungry and wished it was Mommy who would be picking her up and not Mrs. Barnes.

She tossed her backpack onto the bench and then crawled up beside it as her eyes filled with tears. A big boy walked past her, staring at the look on her face. Embarrassed, she drew her knees up under her chin and hid her face.

"Hey there, are you all right?"

At the touch on her shoulder, Hope flinched, and then looked up. There was a very tall man kneeling on the ground in front of her. Instinctively, she pulled away and looked nervously toward her teacher, Mrs.

Kristy. But Mrs. Kristy had not realized that Hope was out of line and was busy with the other students.

"It's okay," the man said. "I just saw you crying and wondered if you were hurt."

"I'm not supposed to talk to strangers," Hope said.

The man smiled and Hope thought he looked like a real clown with his wide, thick lips and the funny little spaces between his teeth. Interested, in spite of her fear, she sat when she should have been moving away.

Howard Lee resisted the urge to laugh. With little girls, it was so easy. It was always so easy. They were born with an innate sense of wanting to please.

"Well, you're right of course. You should never talk to strangers who might hurt you. But I'm not going to do that, am I?"

Hope shrugged, her gaze still riveted on the way his tongue brushed against the inside of his teeth as he talked.

"You know what?" Howard Lee asked.

Hope shook her head.

"You look like a little girl who's about to have a birthday. Am I right?"

Hope's eyes widened as she nodded. She was inordinately proud of the fact that she would soon be seven and a year older than a lot of the kids in her class.

"I thought so!" Howard Lee said, and clapped his hands together, as if in quick delight. "I'll bet you're having a party, aren't you? Going to invite all your friends and play games and eat cake and ice cream."

Hope's expression fell. "I don't think so," she said.

Howard Lee's mouth turned downward, giving his expression a sudden mournful look. He wanted to touch her, but knew it was far too soon. However, he couldn't resist a quick touch to her hair as he stroked a finger down the length of one curl.

"Why, that's just awful," he said. "A little girl as pretty as you should have a party...lots of parties, in fact."

Instinct kicked in as Hope retreated from the intrusion of his touch. She grabbed her backpack and slid from the bench just as her teacher suddenly realized she was missing.

Lena Kristy saw the familiar blue van pulling up at the curb and looked around for Hope O'Rourke. She frowned when she realized she was no longer in line, but when she turned around to search for her and saw her talking to a stranger, her frustration turned to fear.

"Hope! Hope! Please come here!"

Hope bolted, relieved that the responsibility of conversation had been removed. She saw Mrs. Barnes and headed for the van, but her teacher stopped her before she could get in.

"Who was that man you were talking to?" Lena asked.

Hope shrugged. "I don't know."

"Where did he come from, dear?"

"I was crying. I didn't see."

Lena squatted down beside the little girl and then cupped her chin.

"Why were you crying, dear? Are you ill?"

"No," Hope said.

"Did someone hurt you?"

"No."

"You had to be crying for a reason. Can't you tell me what it was?"

"Mrs. Barnes wasn't here. I don't like it when she's late. It makes me sad."

Lena sighed and gave Hope a quick hug. Anxiety was hard to deal with, especially when you're only six.

"But she's here now, isn't she?" Lena said. "So off you go, and if you see that man again, you run and tell me. It's not okay to talk to him."

Hope nodded.

Lena ushered the child into the van and then turned around, searching the schoolyard for the man she'd seen, but he was no longer in sight. Anxious to report to her principal, she hustled the other children into their parents' cars and then headed for the school building. Two little girls had already gone missing in Savannah and she wasn't taking any chances. While these children were in her care, they were her babies.

"Mommy, it's not okay to talk to strangers, is it?" Hope asked.

The curious inflection in Hope's voice made Mary's skin crawl. She dropped the potato she was peeling into the sink, wiped her hands on a towel and then turned to look at her daughter, who was sitting at the kitchen table. Her head was bent toward her coloring book, the cookie Hope had given her earlier was gone, and her glass of milk was half-empty. It was an innocent scene, but the question Hope asked was not.

"No, it's not okay," Mary said. "Why do you ask?"

Hope shrugged and discarded her red crayon for a blue one.

Mary sat down in the chair across from Hope and for a moment, simply watched the intensity on her daughter's face. As she sat, it occurred to her that fear was not something she would have expected in heaven, and with that came the thought that her theory could be horribly flawed. If so, then she wasn't dead, but if she wasn't dead, then where was she?

It wasn't the first time today that she'd experienced something disturbing, but this was the worst. And while she had no explanation for what was going on in her life, the reality of her "here and now" was too vivid to explain away as a dream.

"Did a stranger talk to you today?"

Without looking up, Hope nodded.

"Where, honey? At dance class?"

"No," Hope said, and abandoned the blue crayon for a yellow one.

Mary sighed. If only she was more confident about this parenting business. She'd only had three months of practice at it before everything had come to an end, and even though she felt a natural and enduring love for this child she was just getting to know, she was uncertain about how to connect.

"Come sit in my lap," Mary asked, and without urging, Hope immediately abandoned her coloring and did as Mary asked.

Mary pulled her close, wrapping her arms around the tiny girl's shoulders and rocking her where they sat.

"Where did you see the stranger?"

"At school." Her features crumpled. "I don't

want to go to dance class with Mrs. Barnes anymore. She's always late. I don't like to be last to go home.''

"Okay, sweetie, we'll talk about dance class later. Right now I need you to tell me more about the man. Did he come to your classroom?"

"No. He was by the gate where we go home."

"Where was Mrs. Kristy?"

Hope hesitated, knowing that it was her fault for getting out of line.

"Honey, you can tell me."

Hope sighed. "I got out of line. Mrs. Barnes wasn't there and I sat on the bench."

Mary's heart sank, thinking how swiftly a child could be lost—and in the place where she should have felt safe.

"Did Mrs. Kristy see him?"

"I don't know. I came when she called me, Mommy. Really I did."

"That's good. Now tell me something else. Were you afraid of him."

Hope shrugged. "I don't know...maybe."

Mary struggled with a sudden fear of her own, knowing that someone they didn't know had violated her daughter's naivety.

"Did he touch you?" Mary asked, and heard the tremble in her own voice.

Hope nodded.

Oh God. Oh God. "Where did he touch you, baby?"

"On my hair. He said I was pretty." At this point, Hope looked up. "Am I, Mommy? Am I pretty?"

Mary made herself smile, but she couldn't talk. Not yet. Not while the taste of bile was so rancid in her mouth.

"He looked like a clown," Hope said.

For a moment, Mary started to relax. A clown. There had been a clown at school—probably in another classroom. It was okay after all.

"Oh...a clown! Did he have a funny costume?"

Hope frowned. "He wasn't a real clown, Mommy. He just looked like one. He had yellow hair and a big mouth with holes between his teeth."

"Holes?"

"Yes, you know...like this."

"Oh! You mean spaces...like his teeth didn't touch each other good."

"Yes. Like that," Hope said.

"What else did he say to you?" Mary asked.

"I don't remember. Mommy, can I go outside and play until Daddy comes home?"

Mary hesitated and then nodded an okay. "But only in the backyard with the fence."

Hope rolled her eyes. "Oh, Mommy. I never play outside my fence. You know that."

Mary made herself laugh, but she felt like crying as Hope bounced off her lap and bolted out the back door. She followed her to the porch, assuring herself that she was right where she'd said she'd be, and then went back inside to finish peeling potatoes.

From the window above the sink, she could see Hope swinging on her swing and sliding down the slide, but it wasn't enough to alleviate the sick feeling in her stomach. And all the while the realization kept growing that she wasn't in heaven after all.

Chapter 6

Daniel's steps were weary as he entered the house, but his spirits lifted as he heard laughter and smelled the welcoming scents of their evening meal. He laid his briefcase on the hall table and then headed for the kitchen. He wanted to shower and change into some comfortable clothes, but he needed to see his girls first.

"I'm home," he yelled, and grinned to himself when he heard his daughter squeal.

"Daddy!" she shrieked, and launched herself toward him, knowing full well he would catch her before she fell.

"Wow," Daniel said, as he hugged her close. "That's quite a welcome. What did I do to deserve that?"

"'Cause you're my Daddy, that's why."

Daniel laughed and pretended to pinch at her nose, then looked over her shoulder toward Mary. She was trying to smile, but he could tell by the look on her face that something was amiss.

"Honey?"

She shook her head and then looked at Hope. He nodded in understanding as Mary spoke.

"Supper is ready, but you have time to change if you want."

He set Hope down and then gave her a playful swat as she dashed toward the kitchen. As soon as Hope was out of hearing, he took Mary in his arms.

"Talk to me."

"Hope said there was a stranger at the schoolyard gates who told her she was pretty. She said he touched her hair."

Daniel's heart stopped, and when it kicked back into rhythm, pounded erratically against his chest.

"God in heaven...where was her teacher?"

"Where she always was, but Hope said she got out of line because she was sad. I don't think Mrs. Kristy knew for a while. Hope also said that Mrs. Barnes wasn't there when school let out. She said she doesn't want to go to dance classes with her anymore because she's always late."

Daniel felt sick to his stomach, absorbing the horror of what he was hearing. At the same time, he thought of the headlines in this morning's paper.

"Two little girls have already been abducted here in the city."

"What?"

Daniel frowned. "Honey...you knew that. We talked about it just last week."

Mary couldn't wrap her thoughts around what she was hearing. The only *last week* she could remember was working as a sales clerk in the dress shop and going home to an empty house.

"Yes, of course," she muttered. "I wasn't thinking."

"Have you talked to Mrs. Kristy?"

Mary flushed. Suddenly she felt as if she'd failed at her duty at a parent.

"No, but Hope only told me about it less than an hour ago. I wanted to talk to you first before I did anything."

"Yes, of course," Daniel said, and then hugged Mary close. "Maybe we're making too much out of nothing, but in this day and age, you can't be too careful."

"That's what I thought," Mary said. "I didn't want to panic and cause Hope to have anxiety. She was already bothered by the fact that in talking to him, she'd disobeyed a very important rule."

"Lord," Daniel muttered, and shoved a hand through his hair. "I'm going to shower and change. Give me five minutes and then I'll be down to supper. We'll call Mrs. Kristy together after Hope goes to bed, okay?"

"Okay," Mary said, and then hugged Daniel tight. "Oh Daniel, when she started talking about that man…" Then she shuddered. "I've never been so scared."

"You did the right thing, honey. Don't worry. Chances are the incident was innocent, but we can never be too careful. She's not even seven years old and still so trusting. Losing her innocence will be inevitable, but not now. Keeping this low-key is the best for her. We don't want to frighten her unnecessarily."

Mary nodded, then watched Daniel bound up the stairs before she went back into the kitchen where Hope was playing. She kept going over and over the sequence of events during the past few hours, certain there was something obvious she was missing, but for the life of her, she couldn't figure out what it was.

She continued to set the table and dish up the food as Hope finished coloring her picture. She was putting ice in their glasses when Hope slapped the coloring book closed and announced.

"Mommy, I'm hungry."

Mary's stomach was in knots as she turned to face her daughter, then she heard Daniel's footsteps as he came hurrying down the stairs.

"Daddy's coming now," Mary said. "Go wash your hands while I put the food on the table, okay?"

"Yea!" Hope cried, and skipped toward the bathroom off the kitchen.

Daniel entered as Hope was leaving. "Yes... Yea! I echo her sentiments," he said. "I'm starving, too."

"After all that shrimp scampi we had at lunch?"

Daniel grinned. "I'm a growing boy."

Mary laughed and handed him a bowl of mashed potatoes.

"Please put these on the table while I get the meat-loaf out of the warming oven."

"Man, I love your meatloaf," Daniel said, as he set the potatoes on the table.

"Salad is in the fridge," Mary said. "Would you get it, too?"

Daniel went toward the refrigerator just as Hope came back in the room.

"May I have juice, please?

"And juice for the princess," Daniel said, as he took a pitcher of apple juice from the refrigerator along with the salad.

Hope sat down at the table with all the assurance of a child who knows she is loved.

"Daddy…"

"What honey?"

"I talked to a stranger today."

Daniel glanced at Mary and then sighed. "I know. Mommy told me."

"I'm sorry."

He put the salad and juice on the table and then sat down beside her.

"Want to talk about it?"

She ducked her chin. "I won't do it again."

Daniel laid his hand on her head, thinking as he did, that for such a small child, she had a very huge hold on his heart.

"That's good, honey." He hesitated, then added. "If you ever see the man again, do you know what to do?"

Hope frowned. "Run away?"

"That's right. Run away, then find your teacher and tell her. Can you remember to do that?"

Hope nodded.

Daniel grinned, and tweaked her nose.

"Good girl." Then he winked at Mary as she set a platter of meatloaf on the table. "Let's eat, what do you say?"

"Yes," Hope said. "I say eat, too."

Mary slid into her seat and bowed her head as Daniel started to say grace, but even as her eyes were closing, she was picturing a man with yellow hair, a big mouth and funny teeth touching her daughter and

telling her she was pretty. It was all she could do not
to throw up.

Lena Kristy was just getting out of the shower
when her phone began to ring. She grabbed for a
towel, wrapping it around her as she raced for the
phone.

"Hello?"

"Mrs. Kristy, it's Daniel O'Rourke. I know this is
an imposition to be calling you at this hour, but
we've had a little situation at home today that you
might be able to help us with."

Lena sat down on the side of the bed. Something
told her she knew what he was going to say before
it came out of his mouth.

"I had a dentist appointment after school today
and I haven't been home very long. I was just getting
out of the shower when you called. Actually, you've
beat me to the punch, because I intended to call
you."

Daniel waved to Mary to pick up the portable
phone so that they could both hear at the same time.

"My wife is on the other phone," Daniel said.

"Hello, Mrs. O'Rourke. Is Hope okay?"

"Yes...but why do you ask?"

"I don't know why *you're* calling, but I know why
I was going to call you."

"Why is that?" Daniel asked.

"When it was time to go home today, I took the
kids out to catch their rides, just like I do every day.
They walk in line and know they're not supposed to
step away, but Hope did. I don't know how long
she'd been out of line when I missed her, but I saw
her even as I was turning to look for her. She was

sitting on that bench just to the left of the gates. You know the one I mean.''

Mary frowned. She could almost picture the school building, but not quite. It was in her memory, but faded, like looking at the world through a thin veil of fog.

''The bench under the trees?'' Daniel asked.

''Yes, that's the one,'' Lena said. ''Anyway, when I saw her, she wasn't alone. There was a man talking to her that I didn't know. I immediately called to Hope and she came running as the man walked away. I never did get a good look at his face, but I do know that he had no business on the grounds. He wasn't a substitute teacher because I checked. We only had two today and they were both women. I told the principal immediately and she called the police, but the man was gone. I can't say that he meant her any harm, but he had no business being there.''

Daniel sighed and rolled his eyes at Mary. They both knew how hectic it was for teachers after school, trying to get the children in the right cars and on the right buses. He could see how the incident had happened, but it didn't make them feel any better.

''I appreciate the fact that you've already taken steps to increase security at school, especially considering the children who've already gone missing here in Savannah.''

Lena sighed. ''I'm so sorry. She's my responsibility and I know it, but sometimes there's not enough of me to go around.''

''I know the feeling,'' Mary said.

''Oh,'' Lena said. ''One more thing. Hope cried today after school. The woman who takes her to

dance class is often late and it makes Hope very anxious. She worries a lot. I just thought you would want
to know.''

"Yes, she told me as much," Mary said. "Daniel
and I haven't talked about it yet, but as far as I'm
concerned, Mrs. Barnes will not be picking Hope up
again. In fact, I'm thinking about taking her out of
the dance class altogether. She's too young to be doing so much, especially during the school week.''

Daniel watched the intensity on Mary's face and
marveled at how far she'd come from the shy, inhib-
ited woman she'd once been.

"I agree," Daniel said. "We'll take care of the
dance class situation and you make sure that man
does not get access to the children again.''

"Consider it already done," Lena said. "The principal assured me that there would be uniformed po-
licemen on duty before and after school until the person responsible for the missing children is found.''

"That's great," Daniel said. "Thanks again for
your help.''

"And thank you for your understanding," Lena
said.

They hung up, then looked at each other and
sighed.

"It isn't easy being a parent, is it?" Mary asked.

Daniel opened his arms. "Come here, baby. I'm
thinking I need a hug.''

Mary's lower lip quivered as she walked into his
arms. "I don't know what I need, but I'm so thankful
you're here with me.''

"Where else would I be?" Daniel asked.

Mary hid her face against his chest and resisted
the urge to roll her eyes. She wanted to tell Daniel

how confused she was. She needed to say aloud everything that was happening to her, but if she did, he would probably have her committed.

Howard Lee took the carton of ice cream out of the grocery sack and put it in the freezer. He'd debated for a good thirty minutes before choosing the flavor, but had finally decided on vanilla. You never went wrong with vanilla. Besides, he had several kinds of sprinkles from which his little angel could choose. Tomorrow he would order her a cake. Strawberry cream, he thought. Pink—for little girls.

He put up the other groceries and then moved to the utility room, took the clean sheets out of the dryer and hurried down the hall to the guest room. He was smiling in anticipation as he began to put the new linens on the bed. The sheets were pink with caricatures of Barbie imprinted upon the fabric. Howard Lee prided himself on being the perfect host, and nothing was too good for his little angels. Each one got their own special sheets for the sleepover, just like they got their own presents for the party. He'd had the Little Mermaid for Amy Anne, but she'd done nothing but cry and beg to go home. Unfortunately, he'd had to resort to stern measures to contain her rebellion.

When he'd adopted Justine, the theme in the guest room had been Cinderella. He'd even gotten a small, stuffed mouse for her to sleep with, reminiscent of the ones in the Disney movie. But she'd tried to crawl out the window, so he had to resort to sedatives in her food and move her down below, just as he now did Amy Anne.

But his hopes were high for his new little girl.

Maybe she would be the one who would settle right in, and when she did, the others would surely follow.

He hummed beneath his breath as he worked, reveling in the sensuousness of the smooth new sheets and the colorful pillow slips on the pillows. Impulsively, he picked up one of the pillows, lifted it to his face then inhaled. Meadow fresh. His favorite scent.

"Perfect," he said, as he laid it against the headboard, then pulled the eyelet bedspread over the sheets and tucked it in place.

His gaze swept the room as he backed out of the doorway, making sure that everything was perfect for his little angel's arrival. His pulse kicked erratically as he gripped the doorknob and then closed the door. Only a few more days and then she'd be here. For Howard Lee, it would be none too soon.

Daniel sat on the side of the bed, watching Mary sleep. This was the second time he'd been up to check on Hope, making sure she was still safe in her bed. He couldn't get past the gut-wrenching fear of knowing he could not protect her every minute of her day.

Mary moaned, then murmured something beneath her breath that Daniel couldn't hear, but he didn't have to hear the words to know the source of her discomfort. He'd seen the panic on her face. He'd heard her voice tremble and her hands shake. A threat to a child, however impotent, was enough to awaken every violent tendency a parent might have.

He sighed, then stretched out beside Mary and took her in his arms.

"Sssh," he whispered, and spooned her against

his body. "It's okay, honey, everything's okay. Just sleep."

Within seconds, he felt her body relaxing, and then heard her breathing even out. Now if he could just follow his own orders, maybe they'd both get some sleep.

Detective Reese Arnaud poured himself a fresh cup of coffee and then headed back to his desk. Last night in Savannah had been a slow night for crime. One hit-and-run without a fatality and a hooker who was claiming rape and assault, along with another crash and grab and two robberies—one at an all-night service station and the other at an ATM.

But he would have willingly worked a night in hell if only they could find the two little girls who'd gone missing last month. Amy Anne Fountain and Justine Marchand were their names—ages six and seven, respectively. Their parents called him every day, and every day he had to tell them that they were still checking out leads. But the truth was, they had no new leads—nothing to lead the police as to where they'd gone or even a hint of who'd taken them.

He took his coffee with him as he headed for the morning meeting where the task force was assembled. Being lead detective on the case made him ultimately responsible for the success or failure of the investigation. It also made him sick to his stomach.

As he walked into the room, his gaze went immediately to the pictures of the two missing victims. The sight of their innocent faces was the stuff of his recent nightmares. What kind of maniac does it take to mess with babies? Tiny little girls whose lives should still be far removed from the ugliness of what the adult world had become. He had nightmares, imagining them crying for their mothers, begging to go home. And that was a best-case scenario. In the real hell that had become his dreams, they were no longer able to cry about anything.

"What do we have?" he asked, "and for God's sake give me some good news."

"Sorry, Arnaud, no can do."

"Then what can you tell me?"

"Well...we're not sure how this connects, or even if it does, but the principal at Robert E. Lee elementary school reported a strange man on the grounds yesterday afternoon."

Arnaud's heart skipped a beat. "Did anybody get a good look at him?"

"Just the kid he was talking to."

"By any chance was it a little girl?"

"Yeah, I think so. Let me check my notes...yeah, here it is. Hope O'Rourke, age six. Her parents are Daniel and Mary O'Rourke."

Arnaud's belly turned. *Ah God...not that Hope.* Pretty, dark-haired, impish little fairy of a female who just happened to be his daughter's best friend.

"God Almighty," Arnaud murmured. Suddenly this was too close to home.

The detective looked up, surprised by Arnaud's reaction.

"You know her?"

"She's Molly's best friend. She's spent the night at my house more than once." Then he managed a small smile. "Hell, once she even threw up on my shoe."

"Man...that's cold," the detective said. "What do you want us to do?"

"I'll do the follow-up," Arnaud said. "She knows me, so chances are if there's anything to tell, I'll get more out of her than anyone else. As for the rest of you, I want unmarked cars at every elementary school this afternoon. Tate...you're point man to co-ordinate with the schools. Make sure the administration knows you're there and why, but keep it low-key. I don't want anyone blowing your covers."

"You got it," Tate said.

Arnaud nodded at the others, glanced one last time at Amy Anne Fountain and Justine Marchand's pictures, then walked out of the room. Whatever it took, he would make sure that Hope O'Rourke's picture did not wind up on there, too.

Daniel's secretary knocked on his door and then stepped inside.

"I know you didn't want to be disturbed, but there's a policeman on the phone who says he needs to talk to you. Line two."

Daniel grabbed the receiver.

"This is Daniel O'Rourke."

"Dan...Reese Arnaud. We need to talk."

Daniel frowned. "What about?"

"We got a report that your daughter was approached yesterday by a stranger on the grounds of her school."

"Since when do homicide detectives investigate those kinds of reports?"

"Since two little girls about her age have gone missing," Arnaud answered.

For a moment, Daniel felt like throwing up, and then he took a deep breath and made himself concentrate.

"Do you think the man Hope saw is the same one who snatched the two girls?"

"I don't know, but at this point, I can't afford to ignore any lead, no matter how small."

Daniel closed his eyes and wearily pinched the bridge of his nose. "What do you want to know?"

"I need to talk to Hope. I want to know what the guy looked like...if she'd ever seen him before. You know...stuff that might give us a lead toward finding the missing children." He paused, then added. "I don't sleep anymore. I find myself getting up at night and going into Molly's room just to make sure she's all right. When they told me about the incident at the school, my first thought was, hell yes...a new lead. And then they told me the child's name and I felt sick to my stomach. Damn it, Daniel, she's Molly's best friend. I've read bedtime stories to her, put Band-Aids on her boo-boos and given up the last of the chocolate chip cookies to her endearing pleas. She's as close to my child as she could be and not be of my blood. I guess what I'm saying is...this hit too close to home."

Daniel stood abruptly and walked to the windows overlooking downtown Savannah, making himself concentrate on the traffic and not the fear in the man's voice, because it made his own far more vivid—and too real. For a while, he'd almost convinced himself that he and Mary had overreacted last night. But this put a whole new color on the incident. If Reese Arnaud was interested, Hope might really be in danger.

"Just tell me what you want and it's yours," Daniel said.

"I need to talk to Hope, but I don't want to scare

her. Do you think it would be all right if I came over after school? I want to bring a sketch artist with me. I know it's a long shot, but it's more than we've had in days.''

"Yes, sure. I'll call Mary."

"Good. I'll be there around four, okay?"

"We'll be waiting."

"Don't say anything to Hope about my coming by," Reese added. "She left a jacket at my house the last time she spent the night. I'll just bring it by and then go from there."

"Yes, okay…I see what you mean."

"This may be nothing," Reese said. "You need to know that at the outset. But I've got two sets of grieving parents who want to know where their babies are, and if Hope can help, I can't pass it up."

"I didn't sleep last night, either. I kept going into Hope's room time and again, just to make sure she was safe in bed. I can't imagine the horror of not knowing where she was or what had happened to her. Bring your sketch artist. Stay as long as you need."

Howard Lee stepped out of the shower and reached for a towel to dry himself off. He'd just gotten home from his shift at the hospital and not for the first time, it occurred to him that working the midnight shift was not conducive to parenthood. He didn't like leaving the girls alone after dark, but at the present time he had no choice. And, until they settled down into the adoption a little better, he could hardly send them off to school and trust them to come home.

He finished drying and then reached for his pajamas, anxious to get in bed. Even though the sun was up and the day was promising to be wonderful, he had to get his rest.

He walked out of the bathroom, then paused, staring down at the throw rug beside his bed. He thought of his girls and wondered what they were doing. His eyelids burned from lack of sleep, but his conscience tugged. A parent should spend quality time with the children, no matter what the cost.

With a heartfelt sigh, he kicked the throw rug aside and then unlocked the padlock on the cellar door. The hinges squeaked a bit as he raised it up, and he made a mental note to oil them. He heard a series of scuffling noises and then nothing.

"Girls...do you want Daddy to come down and play for a while?"

There was a long and pregnant moment of utter silence, then what sounded like a muffled sob. He frowned.

"Stop crying, damn it!" he yelled, and slammed the door shut with a bang, then locked it and kicked the throw rug in place.

He yanked back his covers and crawled into bed, too tired to deal with the situation. The sheets were clean and cool, just like his mother had always insisted they should be. It prided him to know that he'd kept the house in the same condition it had always been when his mother had been alive.

Despite the sunlight beaming through the curtains, he closed his eyes and slept.

Justine Marchand had turned seven two months ago, but she was small for her age. She had straight, dark hair, big brown eyes and a slight pout to her rosebud mouth. There were exactly four tiny brown

freckles on the bridge of her nose and she liked
Mickey Mouse and the PowerPuff girls. When she
grew up, she wanted to be a nurse.

And somewhere between the morning she'd left
for school and before she'd gone home, she'd been
thrust into hell. She didn't understand exactly what
was happening, but she wanted to go home.

When the cellar door had opened, she'd grabbed
Amy Anne and crawled under the bed. Even though
she knew the man would eventually make her come
out, it still seemed plausible to resist in every way
she dared. She wasn't supposed to talk to strangers,
but she was stuck with him, just the same.

However, he hadn't come down as she'd feared,
and when he yelled at her and then slammed the
door, she went weak with relief. She didn't care how
loud he yelled, as long as he stayed away. He smiled
too much and was always touching her face and her
hair.

As soon as it was quiet, she crawled out from under the bed, pulling Amy Anne with her, then
smoothed the hair away from the other girl's face.

"He's gone now," she said, and led Amy Anne
to the little table in the middle of the room. "Want
to color in the color books or watch TV?"

Amy Anne didn't answer. Justine wasn't even sure
she could talk. She hadn't said a word since she'd
been here. She didn't even know if the girl belonged
to the man, or if she was lost, too.

"We'll color," she said softly, and sat the little
girl in a chair. "That way we won't make any noise
and wake him up."

She opened a coloring book for herself, then
opened one for Amy Anne.

"Here," she said. "You can have the blue crayon and I'll pick red."

She put the crayon in Amy Anne's lifeless hands and waited for her to move. It didn't happen.

"It's okay," she finally said, and patted Amy Anne on the head. "You can watch me, instead."

She picked up the red crayon and then started to cry, softly, so that no one could hear.

"I want to go home, Amy Anne. I don't like it here."

Chapter 7

Mary had started out dusting the bookshelves in the living room, but now the dust cloth and furniture polish was sitting idle on a nearby table and she was cross-legged in the floor with a picture album in her lap. Nothing could have prepared her for what she'd found inside, not even the wildest of dreams.

The first pages were devoted to the first year of her and Daniel's marriage. She remembered those times and the pictures being taken. The pictorial mementos moved from there to Hope's birth, and then the first three months of her life. Most of them consisted of pictures of Daniel holding Hope, or Daniel's parents holding Hope. The images were burned in her mind.

But then she'd turned the next page and faced a truth that was impossible to deny. Page after page, year after year, were pictures of Mary with Hope, and Mary with Daniel, physical proof that she'd been present during all these events. They were nonsensical pictures, the kind that were precious only to the people taking them, ranging in ordinary diversity from braiding Hope's hair to building a sand castle at the beach. Pictures of Christmases past and the first Thanksgiving in their new house, her thirtieth birthday and Daniel giving her the keys to her new car. The more she looked, the more it seemed she remembered. But it made no sense. How could she remember something that hadn't happened?

Then she sighed and rubbed the worry spot between her eyebrows. What on earth was she asking? This had to be more of her increasing insanity. More than once during the past twenty-four hours she'd wondered if she was actually locked up in some hospital somewhere and only living out this fantasy in her mind. It made more sense than anything else she could think of. Then she looked back at the pictures. It just all seemed so real.

Many times over the past six years she'd wished for the ability to turn back time—to relive that moment when Daniel had put Hope in the car and then started to back out of the driveway into the path of that high-speed pursuit. She'd relived that horror over and over every time she'd closed her eyes, but it had always been the same. The fight—Hope crying—Daniel leaving in anger—and her watching them driving away without trying to make him stop.

The flesh suddenly crawled on the back of her neck. It had always been the same.

Until yesterday.

Yesterday in the antique store she'd had the same dream, and it had not changed—until the point where Daniel started to back out of the drive. This time she'd thrown herself on the hood of the car instead of watching him drive away. This time she had screamed for him to stop, then begged him not to leave—and for the first time since the nightmare had begun, he and Hope had lived.

She closed her eyes, remembering the ring that she'd found in that old scrap of lace—and the odd little man who'd looked at her with such sad, sad eyes. The ring had been so small and yet it had slid upon her finger as if it had been made to fit. She took a deep breath, making herself calm and trying to remember what had happened next.

Oh yes—the scent of dust was in the air and another, more subtle scent of faded roses. She'd started to feel faint and reached out to steady herself against a counter.

Mary's heart started to pound. Even now she could feel the heart-stopping panic of knowing something had been set into motion that she could not stop. She vaguely remembered how her head had started to spin, as if everything she was looking at was turning backward.

Backward!

She gasped as a new thought occurred.

Backward?

No. Not that.

It wasn't possible.

There was no such thing as going back in time.

But she couldn't turn loose of the notion. What if that last dream she'd had of their fight had been real? What if she really had been given the opportunity to change their fates? What if she *had* saved their lives and changed the future?

She shoved the picture album back on the shelf

and got to her feet, then went to the phone, picked up the receiver and dialed the operator.

"Operator, how may I help you?"

"What's today's date?"

"I'm sorry?" the operator said.

"Please," Mary pleaded. "Just tell me. What's today's date?"

"September 26th."

Mary started to shake. She'd walked into the antique store on October 2nd. She took a deep breath and then asked.

"What's the year?"

"Ma'am, are you ill?"

No, but I may be crazy. "No, just please tell me. What year is this?"

"It's September the 26th, 2002."

Mary replaced the receiver without acknowledgment of the operator's last answer. What was there to say? *Oh, by the way, I think I've traveled backward in time and don't want to be late for dinner?*

Before she could follow the thought any further, the phone rang. She jerked back in reflex, half expecting to hear the operator's voice telling her to get ready for a permanent trip to the funny farm.

"Hello?"

"Mary, darling, how are you?"

"Phyllis?"

Phyllis O'Rourke laughed. "Yes, it's me. Surely it hasn't been *that* long since we talked."

Only six years…but who's counting. "Sorry, I was sort of preoccupied."

"I certainly know how that is," Phyllis said. "As for the reason I'm calling, it will soon be Hope's birthday. I wanted to know if you'd made any special plans, because if not, Mike and I would love to have all of you over for dinner.''

"That sounds wonderful," Mary said. "I'll check with Daniel and get back to you, okay?"

"Great! I wasn't sure if you would be having a party for her or not, and certainly don't want to intrude.''

"Grandparents never intrude," Mary said.

"You're a dear," Phyllis said. "I'd love to chat longer but Mike is waiting for me. Let me know about the dinner later. Bye-bye.''

"Yes, goodbye," Mary said, and hung up, amazed that the conversation with a woman who had once hated her guts seemed so comfortable and warm.

She started back to the photo albums when the phone suddenly rang again. This time she was a little more composed.

"Hello?"

"Hey, good-looking…it's me.''

Relief washed over her in waves and sent her moving backward toward a chair.

"Oh…it's you.''

She heard amusement in his voice.

"Who did you think it would be?''

"I just finished talking to your mom. She invited us to dinner for Hope's birthday.''

"What did you tell her?''

"That I'd get back to her later after I talked to you.''

"Whatever you want is fine with me," Daniel said. "Are you busy?''

"Not really. I was looking at old photo albums

when Phyllis called and was still standing by the phone when it rang. It startled me.''

He chuckled. ''Hey, honey…I don't have long before I have to be in court, but the reason I called is that Reese Arnaud telephoned. He wants to talk to Hope about the man who approached her at school yesterday.''

''Reese Arnaud?''

Daniel frowned. These blank spots in Mary's memory were beginning to trouble him.

''Molly's father? Hope's best friend, Molly? He's a detective with the Savannah P.D., remember?''

Mary's stomach knotted. ''The police. Oh God…yes…of course, I'd forgotten he was with the police. Oh Daniel, do they think—''

''They don't think anything right now, honey. They're just covering all the bases. With those two little girls still missing, they can't afford to ignore anything, even if it's a long shot, okay?''

''Yes, of course. What do I do?''

''Pick Hope up from school as usual, then go straight home. He's coming over at four on the pretext of bringing back a jacket that she left at their house the last time she spent the night with Molly. He's bringing a sketch artist, too, but let him handle all the explanations. Hope won't think anything of Reese coming there, and he knows how to talk to her without frightening her.''

Mary's voice was shaking. She knew it, but she couldn't make it stop.

''Will you be here?''

''You couldn't keep me away.''

Mary sighed. ''This is awful, isn't it?''

"Yes, but not as awful as what the parents of those two missing children are going through."

"Oh, Daniel…"

"Hang in there, honey. Hope's safe and we're going to make sure she stays that way."

Howard Lee took the two bowls of macaroni and cheese from the microwave and put them on a tray, then added two plastic spoons and two snack-size fruit juices in disposable packs. He stared at the tray for a moment and then moved to the sideboard, took a couple of bananas from a bowl and added them to the tray.

"There now…a perfectly good lunch for growing girls."

He picked up the tray and headed down the hall, then into his own bedroom. Nudging the door closed with the toe of his shoe, he set the tray down on the bed, then shoved aside a small area rug, revealing the metal door on the floor. He lifted it, letting it rest against the side of the bed as he turned for the tray and started down the stairs.

Ignoring the fact that he'd yelled at them earlier, his voice was full of overdone delight.

"Hello, hello, hello," he said, as he began to descend. "I brought you some yummy lunch. Are my two little angels hungry?"

Amy Anne Fountain had once been a happy, smiling little girl, but there was little left of the child that she'd been. Even though her clothes were spotless and her long brown hair had been brushed and clipped away from her face with a bright red bow, the bruises on her arms and the cut on her lip were impossible to miss. She was sitting on the side of the bed, her stare blank, a spittle of drool barely visible at the edge of her lower lip.

Justine Marchand had been an impish, outgoing child who'd never met a stranger. Then she'd met Howard Lee Martin, and the name "stranger" had taken on a whole different meaning. She'd been putty in his hands from the very first and had never seen the danger coming. He'd used the "puppy on a leash" trick, waited until he'd seen her coming, then dropped the leash, knowing full well that the puppy would bolt. Justine had seen the puppy coming at her, seen the funny man running after the puppy as hard as he could go, and thought she was doing a good deed. Only four blocks from her home she'd gotten down on her knees and caught the puppy in her arms. She was smiling as she'd handed him to the big man, and felt no danger when he'd patted her on the back and thanked her for being so kind.

When he'd offered to let her hold the puppy's leash as they walked toward her home, she'd been distracted by the unexpected treat and had done the unforgivable. She'd walked away with a stranger. She couldn't remember the last time she'd seen her mommy and daddy. She'd quit crying for them at night now and even though Amy Anne didn't talk to her, Justine slept curled around her as if she were a lifeline to sanity.

She heard the door open above them and then the man's voice calling down. She stood abruptly, unwilling to be on the bed. He played games on the bed that she didn't like. Her fingers curled around her friend's wrist as she whispered in desperation.

"Get up, Amy Anne...you have to get up."

But Amy Anne didn't move, and Justine wasn't strong enough to lift her. Helpless to do anything but take care of herself, she ran to the other side of the room.

Mary had started toward Hope's school almost an hour before school was due to be dismissed. Part of it had been fear that she wouldn't know where to go, but more importantly, she never wanted Hope to be anxious again about being picked up. Even though she hadn't known exactly where to go, she'd driven straight to the school without missing a turn. She was starting to accept the fact that something extraordinary had happened to her life. She parked on the street and then leaned back against the seat, willing her pounding heart to ease.

As she waited, she glanced up in the rearview mirror and saw a tall, blond-haired man dressed in jogging clothes coming down the sidewalk. He was walking casually, once stopping to tie his shoe. When he straightened up, he glanced around as if looking to see if he'd been observed.

Mary's fingers curled around the steering wheel. He had blond hair. What if it was the man who'd talked to Hope? She reached for her purse and took out her phone. If he would only come a little closer, she would be able to see his face better.

As she waited, her finger poised to call 9-1-1, a yellow school bus came up behind her, passed where she was waiting, and pulled into line at the curb. At that point, she could no longer see the jogger. Seconds later, a second bus pulled to the curb, then a third and a fourth until the curb was lined with buses waiting to load and her view of the sidewalk was completely blocked.

A couple of drivers got out. One of them lit up a cigarette and started to smoke while another circled his bus, kicking at the tires and checking the back door to make sure it was securely fastened.

Mary got out of her car and moved toward the sidewalk in front of the school, still looking for the man in the jogging suit, but he was nowhere in sight. Then she noticed a uniformed policeman just inside the front gate and began to relax.

At that moment, she heard a loud, strident bell from within the building behind her. Seconds later, the front doors opened and children came spilling out of the schoolhouse and down the steps. Frustration set in as the teachers and the children came toward her. She tried not to panic, but she had absolutely no idea what her own daughter's teacher looked like.

"Hi, Mrs. O'Rourke! Are you looking for Hope?"

Mary turned around, then looked down. A small, blond-haired girl with chubby cheeks was looking up at her, smiling in obvious recognition.

"Yes, I am," she said. "Who are you?"

The little girl laughed out loud, as if Mary had just told her a funny joke.

"It's me, Molly."

Molly. Hope's best friend. "Why, so it is," Mary said, and pretended to rub sleep from her eyes.

Molly laughed again and then pointed behind her.

"There they come now. The last rows had to wait in the hall because Frances Sheffield threw up."

"Oh, my," Mary said.

"Mommy! Mommy!"

Mary turned, saw Hope waving at her from the front of the line, and breathed a huge sigh of relief.

"Hi, honey," she called.

"Mary...good afternoon."

Mary took a calculated guess at the identity of the woman and jumped into the conversation with both feet.

"Hello, Mrs. Kristy. I hear someone had a little accident in the hall."

Lena Kristy rolled her eyes. "Five more seconds and we would have been out of the building, too."

Mary smiled sympathetically as Hope slipped her hand in her mother's palm.

"Mommy, can we go home now?"

Mary looked down at her daughter, her heart filling with a love she would have been hard-pressed to describe.

"Yes, darling...we can go home." She glanced at Mrs. Kristy. "Okay?"

"Very okay," Mrs. Kristy said, then she began loading her children, making sure they got on the proper buses while the other parents who picked up their children still waited in their cars.

Hope was talking nonstop, skipping as she walked, secure that all was right with her world. Mary listened absently, answering only when necessary as they moved toward the car. She kept looking at everyone they passed, as well as the people who waited in cars. Some waved at her. She waved back, assuming she should know who they were.

"Mommy, I'm hungry. Can we stop on the way home for a Slushee?"

Mary thought of the detective who was due soon

at their house. "Not today, Hope. We need to hurry home."

"Why?"

She hesitated. Daniel had told her not to let Hope know Detective Arnaud was coming to talk to her.

"Because...because I think Daddy is coming home early and we don't want to miss him."

"Yea!" Hope cried. "Maybe he'll play ball with me."

Mary smiled. "Maybe...but we'll have to wait and see, okay?"

"Okay."

Howard Lee glared at the presence of the policeman while watching the buses loading from across the street. When the cop looked his way, he picked up the clippers that were lying by the hedge where he was standing and began clipping at the bushes as if he lived there. He'd seen the woman get out of the car and thought nothing of it. There were hundreds of children in that school. What were the odds that she would be there for his angel?

He cut at the shrubbery in short, angry jerks, telling himself it didn't matter—that he still had plenty of time to make the plan work.

He watched the buses pull away and then stepped back into the shade of a magnolia tree as the first of the cars began to depart. He saw her then, in her pretty blue car, all smiling and happy, and his anger spiked. It wasn't fair. This was his little girl. He'd picked her out special. That woman couldn't possibly know how to make a little girl happy. Not like he did. Amy Anne and Justine needed that new sister and he wasn't going to disappoint them. He threw

the clippers down with a curse and then started jogging toward home.

Reese Arnaud pulled up in front of the O'Rourke
house and then reached over in the back seat and got
the little pink jacket that Hope had left at his house.
He eyed the sketch artist, giving him one last re-
minder.

"Okay, Kelly, remember we take this slow. If we
frighten her, it's over."

"Yes, sir," the officer said, and gathered up his
briefcase as he got out of the car.

Reese's focus was on high as he rang the doorbell.
*Please God, let this be the break we've been waiting
for.*

Moments later, the door opened and Mary let them
inside.

Reese hugged her briefly, wanting to allay the fear
he saw on her face.

"Hello, Mary. Sorry that this is happening."

"No more than we are," she said. "Hope is in her
room. I'll call her."

"We need to make this real informal. How about
we set up in the kitchen? Maybe with cookies and
milk?"

Mary smiled. "It will be her second round. Something tells me she won't object."

Reese chuckled. "Yeah, she's hell on chocolate
chip cookies, isn't she?"

Mary nodded, but her thoughts were somewhere
else. *Chocolate chip cookies were her favorites? Another thing I hadn't known.* "Please see yourselves
to the kitchen. We'll be right there."

As she started up the stairs, it occurred to her that

Reese Arnaud probably knew more about her daughter's likes and dislikes than she did. The thought was not only daunting but made her feel lacking as the mother she wanted to be. She headed down the hall and then pushed the door open to Hope's room.

"Hi, Mommy! Is Daddy home yet?"

"No, but you have a visitor."

"Who? Is it Molly?"

"Close, but not Molly."

Abandoning the puzzle she'd been working, Hope jumped up from her little chair and ran out of her room and down the hall.

"Don't run down the stairs," Mary cautioned, then groaned beneath her breath as Hope bounded down the stairs anyway.

Mary hurried down behind her and followed Hope into the kitchen, just in time to hear her cry.

"Uncle Reese…it's you! Did you bring Molly to play with me?"

Reese Arnaud scooped the little girl up into his arms and gave her a quick hug.

"No, but I brought your pink jacket."

"Oh, goody. Is that where it was?"

He grinned. "Yep. I wanted to wear it, but pink's not my color."

Hope giggled. "Uncle Reese, you're so silly. You can't wear my jacket. You're too big."

"Maybe you're right," he said, then pointed to the officer he'd brought with him. "This is my friend, Kelly. We're having cookies and milk. Want to have some with us?"

Hope looked to Mary for permission. When Mary nodded, she wiggled out of Reese's arms and headed for the fridge.

"I'll get my own milk," she said, and dragged a nearly full gallon of milk from the shelf.

"Maybe I'd better help," Mary said, and grabbed the gallon carton from Hope's hands before the milk hit the floor. "Why don't you sit down by Uncle Reese while I get your snack?"

Before Hope could settle, they heard the front door open.

"Daddy's home!" Hope cried. "Daddy! We're in here!" she yelled, and then snagged a cookie from the plate before anyone changed their minds about letting her have a second snack.

Mary nodded at the two officers then went to meet Daniel.

"Sorry I'm late. Got a late phone call I couldn't ignore. Have they started yet?" Daniel asked.

"No, they just got here."

"Good. Give me a second and I'll join you."

He set his briefcase on the floor beside the hall table and then took off his suit coat and hung it on the newel post as they passed the staircase.

As they entered the kitchen, Daniel's gaze met and then slid past Reese Arnaud to the little girl sitting across the table from him.

"Hey, punkin…did you save me any cookies?"

Hope giggled and took another big bite. "Nope."

"You little pig…then I'm going to eat yours," Daniel teased, and grabbed at his daughter's wrist, pretending to eat her cookie.

Reese's nerves were on edge as he waited for the hilarity to cease. He couldn't help thinking about the two missing children—wondering if they were even alive—knowing if they were, they might never laugh again.

Finally, the silliness stopped as Daniel sat at the table and then took Hope on his lap. At his nod, the sketch artist took a pad and charcoal pencil from his briefcase and started to draw. Immediately, Hope's interest shifted.

"What are you doing?" she asked.

Reese leaned forward, his gaze fixed on Hope's face.

"He's going to draw me a picture."

"What kind of a picture?" Hope asked.

"Oh, I don't know, do you have a suggestion?"

Hope grinned. "A horse! Draw a picture of a horse!"

Mary slid into the seat beside Daniel and Hope. She didn't touch them, but she needed to be close. What happened during the next few minutes might be vital to finding the missing children as well as keeping her own daughter safe.

"How about a clown?" Mary asked. "Ask him if he knows how to draw a clown."

Reese already knew that Hope had referred to the stranger at school as looking like a clown. He nodded his approval at Mary for introducing the subject for him.

"That sounds like a good idea," Reese said.

Hope frowned. "I don't think I like clowns."

"Why not?" Reese asked.

Hope leaned back against Daniel's chest, taking comfort in his presence.

"It's okay, honey," Daniel said. "You can tell Uncle Reese."

"I did something bad," she said, and then looked away.

"No, it wasn't bad," Daniel said. "But it was wrong, wasn't it?"

She nodded.

"So, tell me what happened, honey."

"I talked to a stranger at school." Then she added. "I'm not supposed to talk to strangers."

"That's right, children don't talk to strangers, but the stranger did something bad, too, didn't he?"

Hope's eyes widened. It was the first time she'd thought about what had happened from another standpoint.

"What did he do?" she asked.

"He talked to you when your mommy and daddy weren't there. He knew better, but he did it anyway. I need to find that man and tell him not to do that again. Do you think that you could help me?"

"I don't know where he lives," Hope said.

"But you know what he looks like, don't you, honey?"

Hope thought about it a moment, then looked at Daniel and Mary.

"It's okay, honey. Mommy and Daddy want you to help Uncle Reese," Mary said. "Do you think you can?"

"Yes, I can do that."

"Great," Reese said, and gave her nose a tweak. "So come sit in my lap and you can watch Kelly drawing, okay?"

"Yes," Hope said, and slid out of Daniel's lap.

"So, this is how we do it," Reese said, as he settled the little girl in his lap. "I'll ask you questions about what he looked like and Kelly will draw what we tell him to draw."

"Was his face round like a balloon, or more square, like a box?"

"Round," Hope answered immediately. "Just like his eyes. They were big and round, too."

Reese's pulse accelerated. Maybe this was going to work after all.

Chapter 8

Howard Lee took a chunk of raw hamburger from the bowl on the counter, made a third hamburger patty and then put it in the hot skillet beside the other two he already had cooking. He turned down the heat, blithely unaware that his premature meeting with Hope O'Rourke had put himself in danger. A few minutes later he took the meat from the pan and put them on a platter to cool while he began to fix the buns.

Amy Anne liked ketchup on her hamburger. Ketchup and nothing else. Justine like mustard and pickles and wanted her hamburger cut into quarters. He put the burgers onto the plates and then added a handful of chips for each girl.

He hummed as he worked, confident that his growing family was intact. Once the plates were to his liking, he moved to the cabinet, took out a bottle of over-the-counter sleeping medicine and measured a

Play the
"LAS VEGAS" Game
and get
3 FREE GIFTS!

FREE GIFTS!

FREE GIFTS!

1. Pull back all 3 tabs on the card at right. Then check the claim chart to see what we have for you — 2 FREE BOOKS and a gift — ALL YOURS! ALL FREE!

2. Send back this card and you'll receive brand-new Silhouette Intimate Moments® novels. These books have a cover price of $4.75 each in the U.S. and $5.75 each in Canada, but they are yours to keep absolutely free.

3. There's no catch. You're under no obligation to buy anything. We charge nothing — ZERO — for your first shipment. And you don't have to make any minimum number of purchases — not even one!

4. The fact is, thousands of readers enjoy receiving their books by mail from the Silhouette Reader Service™. They enjoy the convenience of home delivery...they like getting the best new novels at discount prices, BEFORE they're available in stores...and they love their *Heart to Heart* newsletter featuring author news, horoscopes, recipes, book reviews and much more!

5. We hope that after receiving your free books you'll want to remain a subscriber. But the choice is yours — to continue or cancel, any time at all! So why not take us up on our invitation, with no risk of any kind. You'll be glad you did!

Visit us online at

www.eHarlequin.com

FREE!
No Obligation to Buy!
No Purchase Necessary!

Play the

"LAS VEGAS" Game

PEEL BACK HERE ▶
PEEL BACK HERE ▶
PEEL BACK HERE ▶

YES! I have pulled back the 3 tabs. Please send me all the free Silhouette Intimate Moments® books and the gift for which I qualify. I understand that I am under no obligation to purchase any books, as explained on the back and opposite page.

345 SDL DNX7   245 SDL DNYE

FIRST NAME	LAST NAME

ADDRESS

APT.#	CITY

STATE/PROV.	ZIP/POSTAL CODE

(S-IM-09/02)

7 7 7		GET 2 FREE BOOKS & A FREE MYSTERY GIFT!
🍀 🍀 🍀		GET 2 FREE BOOKS!
🍒 🍒 🍒		GET 1 FREE BOOK!
🔔 🔔 🔔		TRY AGAIN!

Offer limited to one per household and not valid to current Silhouette Intimate Moments® subscribers. All orders subject to approval.

▼ DETACH AND MAIL TODAY ▶

The Silhouette Reader Service™ — Here's how it works:

Accepting your 2 free books and gift places you under no obligation to buy anything. You may keep the books and gift and return the shipping statement marked "cancel." If you do not cancel, about a month later we'll send you 6 additional novels and bill you just $3.99 each in the U.S., or $4.74 each in Canada, plus 25¢ shipping & handling per book and applicable taxes if any.* That's the complete price and — compared to cover prices of $4.75 each in the U.S. and $5.75 each in Canada — it's quite a bargain! You may cancel at any time, but if you choose to continue, every month we'll send you 6 more books, which you may either purchase at the discount price or return to us and cancel your subscription.

*Terms and prices subject to change without notice. Sales tax applicable in N.Y. Canadian residents will be charged applicable provincial taxes and GST.

If offer card is missing write to: Silhouette Reader Service, 3010 Walden Ave., P.O. Box 1867, Buffalo, NY 14240-1867

BUSINESS REPLY MAIL
FIRST-CLASS MAIL   PERMIT NO. 717-003   BUFFALO, NY

POSTAGE WILL BE PAID BY ADDRESSEE

SILHOUETTE READER SERVICE
3010 WALDEN AVE
PO BOX 1867
BUFFALO NY 14240-9952

NO POSTAGE
NECESSARY
IF MAILED
IN THE
UNITED STATES

small dose into two cups, then filled the cups with milk, adding a dollop of chocolate syrup to make sure the taste of the medicine was masked. He'd never intended to use this method of control, but after the first night with Amy Anne in the guest room, he'd been forced to resort to other measures.

A few minutes later he started down into the cellar. As he did, he heard a scurrying of feet and smiled to himself, knowing that his girls were aware of his imminent arrival.

"Daddy's here," he called, then frowned when there was no welcoming response.

It aggravated him that after all he'd given them and done for them, they still withheld their affections. Even though their room was technically a cellar, he had not spared expenses in outfitting it. Besides the large room that served as living room and bedroom, he'd gone to a lot of trouble to install their own bathroom with tub and shower.

There was a television, a VCR and more than a dozen children's videos for them to watch. There were two white twin-size brass beds against one wall and a wooden table and chairs near the center of the room, piled high with coloring books, crayons and puzzles. As he came down the steps, he noticed that none of the toys had been moved, although the television was on.

Refusing to admit that his plan to create his own family was less successful than he had imagined, he set the tray down on the table and then fixed a place setting at each chair, carefully laying out their plate of food, a napkin, a fork and their cups of chocolate milk.

"Look what Daddy's made for you tonight."

"My daddy doesn't know how to cook," Justine murmured, and slipped into one of the chairs.

Howard Lee frowned. "I'm your Daddy now," he said sharply.

Justine's lower lip trembled and her eyes welled with tears, but she'd learned early on that arguing with the man just made things worse. Without saying anything more, she began nibbling on a potato chip as the man took Amy Anne in his lap and started to feed her.

As usual, ever since she'd been with the man, Amy Anne only sat and stared.

"Eat your hamburger," Howard Lee said.

Justine grabbed one of the pieces and took a big bite, not because she was particularly hungry, but because she didn't want to make the man angry.

"Is it good?" Howard Lee asked.

She nodded.

"Drink all your milk, too."

She eyed the cup of chocolate milk, wishing she had the nerve to tell him she didn't like chocolate in her milk, then thought better of it.

"When can we go outside and play?" Justine asked.

Howard Lee's frown deepened. The dilemma of keeping his family intact was warring with the knowledge that growing children needed fresh air and sunshine.

"After we move. When we get to our new house, then you can go outside, all right?"

The food suddenly knotted in Justine's stomach. She didn't want to go anywhere with the man but back to her real home. She thought of Charlie, her puppy, and her mother and daddy. She wondered if they cried for her like she cried for them.

"I want my mother," Justine muttered, then took another bite.

Ignoring her discontent, Howard Lee shifted Amy Anne to a more comfortable position, then picked up the hamburger and offered her a bite. At his bidding, Amy opened her mouth, accepting the food without acknowledging the giver.

"See, Amy Anne, just like you like it," Howard Lee said. "Is it good?"

Even if she'd been capable of answering, she would have been hard-pressed to tell Howard Lee what he wanted to hear. There was no longer such a thing as "good" in Amy Anne's world.

Hiding his frustration, he dabbed at a dribble of ketchup hanging at the corner of her mouth and then offered her a drink of milk. She drank without purpose, neither acknowledging hunger or thirst, but simply acquiescing to his demands. It wasn't what he wanted, but her withdrawal had left him with no leverage.

"When you finish your food, we need to take our baths and get ready for bed," Howard Lee said.

Justine looked down at her half-eaten burger and wanted to cry. She wanted to play in her yard and sleep in her own little bed. At home, she always slept with her dolly, Freckles. The man had given her a different dolly to sleep with, but it wasn't the same.

"Drink your milk," Howard Lee said.

Afraid of what he might do if she chose to disobey him, she emptied the glass. Within minutes, both she and Amy Anne were asleep where they sat.

Howard Lee smiled to himself in satisfaction as he

began to take off their clothes. It was always easier to bathe them and put on their nightclothes when they were quiet and compliant. He set Amy Anne aside, went into the small bathroom and ran some water in the tub. Then he turned around, looking from one little girl to the other and decided.

"Justine, tonight you can be first."

It was a blessing for the child that the sedation he'd given her had already taken effect. She never knew when he took off her clothes, or carried her into the bathroom and lowered her in the tub. She did not have to suffer the indignity of a stranger's hands upon her body or wonder about the look in his eyes.

Reese Arnaud stared down at the face on the sketch pad, wondering how accurate a child's description was going to be in aiding their investigation. In a way, the image was almost comical. The man Hope described had a wide mouth and thick lips, with short, blond bangs cut straight across his forehead. His big, round eyes were set in an even rounder face. And his teeth. Hope had been adamant about his teeth. The spaces between the teeth were definitely unique. No wonder she'd thought he was a clown.

It dawned on Reese as he fixed the image in his mind that, if the man was the one they were looking for, he might very well be using the oddity of his features to his advantage. Most children loved clowns. What better way to approach a child than with humor?

"So, Hope, what do you think?"

"It's the man, Uncle Reese. It's the man who touched my hair and told me I was pretty."

The connotation behind the words make Reese sick, but he hid his feelings as he leaned forward and gave her a big hug.

"Thank you so much, honey. You've been a big help."

"You're welcome," she said, and then looked up at Mary. "Mommy, may I go outside and play on my swing until supper?"

"Yes."

With the innocence of youth, and unaware of the dangers she had skirted, Hope was out the back door, leaving the adults speechless.

"Just like that," Daniel said.

Mary leaned her head against Daniel's shoulder. "She's little, and thank God, was unaffected by the incident."

Daniel looked at Reese. "What are the odds that the man Hope saw is the man you're looking for?"

Reese shrugged. "Probably far less than we'd like, but we can't afford to ignore anything."

"If there's something else we can do, don't hesitate to ask."

"Will do," Reese said. "Kelly, pack it up. I want to get back to the department and get this out to the officers."

"Are you going to go public with the picture?" Mary asked.

"We can't...at least not yet. If he's who we're looking for, we don't want to give him a chance to run."

"Yes, of course. I wasn't thinking. I just want this man found."

"Thanks to your daughter, it might happen."

Mary walked the two officers to the door and then stopped Reese just before he exited.

"Will you let us know what happens?"

"You know we will."

Mary stood and watched until they drove away. As she started back in the house, a car backfired at the corner of the block. She jumped and spun, her eyes wide and startled. Only after she realized what she'd heard, did she start to relax. She stepped inside, scanning the area with a nervous glance as if she half-expected to find danger lurking nearby, then she shut the door and went back into the kitchen.

Daniel was standing at the window, watching Hope play. She put her arms around his waist and laid her head in the middle of his back. As they stood together in silence, she felt a shudder run through him.

"Daniel?"

"What?"

"What are you thinking?"

"How do we keep her safe?" Then he turned around and took Mary in his arms. "I'm not referring to just this incident. How do we ever let her out of our sight again?"

Mary knew how he felt, but she'd learned the hard way that living in fear was not really living at all.

"We love her with all our hearts, teach her everything we know to help her make the right choices, and after that, Daniel, it's all up to God."

"God? Where was he when those two little girls were taken? Why are men like that allowed to live? Tell me that."

Mary had lived with negative thinking for six years and it had nearly killed her.

"God doesn't do that stuff, Daniel, but he's there to help us through it when it happens."

Daniel sighed. "I know. I didn't mean what I said, it's just that this is scary as hell."

"I know, but for Hope's sake, we've got to keep everything as ordinary as possible."

"Yes, I know you're right, but it's not going to be easy."

Mary slid her arms around his neck and then kissed the small indentation on his chin.

"Who said being a parent was going to be easy?"

Daniel took one look at the expression on Mary's face and groaned beneath his breath.

"Are you thinking what I think you're thinking?"

"Probably, but it's going to have to wait."

"This doesn't have to wait," Daniel said, and slanted his mouth across Mary's lips.

It was just after midnight when Mary woke and found herself alone. She lay there for a moment, listening to the sounds within the house. Somewhere a faucet was dripping. She could hear the occasional plink as the water hit something metal. Outside, a wind had come up, causing one of the limbs of the live oak to rub against the window nearest the bed. The intermittent scratch of wood against glass set her nerves on edge. Still wondering where Daniel had gone, she got out of bed and went across the hall to check on Hope.

The room was dark, lit only by the Little Mermaid nightlight plugged in near her bed. God…six years of her daughter's life that she could barely remember.

She was past wondering how this had happened. That she had them back in her life was all that she would let matter.

A gust of wind rattled the windows across the hall. She looked up just as a streak of lightning slashed through the darkness. One second it was there, brilliant and dangerous in all its fury, and then it was gone. She shivered as she reached for the curtains, pulling them shut and hoping that the approaching storm wouldn't disturb Hope's sleep. Another gust of wind slammed against the house, followed by a second clap of thunder. Hope seemed undisturbed by the noise. Satisfied that her daughter was well, she pulled the covers back over her shoulders and then went in search of Daniel.

The lower level of the house was in shadows, but she thought she felt a draft on her bare feet as she moved through the rooms. Surely a door had been opened, but where? More to the point, she should be asking herself why?

"Daniel?"

She held her breath, waiting for an answer that didn't come. She continued through the house, her anxiety growing as she looked in every room. She hurried into the dining room and tested the French doors on the off chance that he'd gone out the back, but they were still locked.

Anxiety changed to panic as she paused in the living room, trying to focus. What was she missing? He couldn't just disappear.

While she was debating about where to look next, she felt cold air on her feet again and realized the front door was ajar.

Thunder rumbled. As she moved toward the window, another slash of lightning seared the air, momentarily lighting the dark. In that brief moment, she saw someone standing beneath the portico. Another flash of lightning came and went, and in that moment she recognized the set of Daniel's shoulders. Almost weak with relief, she dashed outside and into his arms.

He'd been out here for what seemed like hours, still troubled that his daughter's safety had been breeched and that she was now involved in a police investigation. Mary had cried herself to sleep in his arms and it had been all he could do not to cry with her. His heart ached, he felt sick to his stomach and he was afraid to close his eyes. He was not a violent man, but he didn't want to think about what he'd do if he came face-to-face with the man who'd messed with his child.

The approaching storm mirrored his angry emotions. Turning his face to the wind, he lifted his chin. The force of it almost took his breath away. The first droplets of rain were just starting to fall when he heard the door open behind him. He turned just as Mary burst from the house.

The storm was upon them now, and even though he had been somewhat sheltered by the portico, the blowing wind and rain immediately plastered their clothes to their bodies as she threw herself into his arms.

"Mary, darling...what's wrong?"

"I thought you were gone."

He turned her in his arms, using his body to shelter her from the storm, and ran with her toward the house. Once inside, he shut and locked the door behind them. Almost immediately, she started to shake.

"Sweetheart…talk to me…tell me what's wrong."

"I woke up and couldn't find you. I thought it was over. Just like before."

Daniel frowned. She wasn't making any sense.

"Over? You thought what was over? And what do you mean…like before?"

"Nothing. Never mind. Just love me, Daniel. Don't let me go."

"Come here to me, baby…never doubt me, Mary Faith. Never."

Daniel picked her up and carried her up the stairs. By the time he got to their bedroom, she was shivering from the cold, her nightgown wet and clinging to her body. He set her on her feet and then shut the door behind them. When the tumblers turned in the lock, he took the hem of Mary's gown and lifted it over her head.

She sighed, shuddering slightly from the chill, as well as from want. Her breasts felt heavy, throbbing with a longing echoed low in her belly.

"Daniel…"

"I know, baby…I know."

Rain splattered against the window as Daniel laid her on the bed. When he crawled in beside her, she lifted her arms and pulled him down to her side.

"I love you, Daniel. You will never know how much."

"I love you, too, baby."

"Show me."

Daniel brushed a kiss across her lips and then did as she asked.

Mary watched Daniel's head dipping toward her, saw his lips parting slightly, smelled the rain on their bodies, then closed her eyes and waited to be swept away by passion.

It didn't take long.

Without foreplay. Without warning. Daniel was on top of her and then in her. Mary parted her legs and arched to meet him, and when he started to move, she met him stroke for stroke.

Outside, the storm was passing, but inside, it had just begun. Daniel had long since lost focus on anything but the feel of being inside his Mary Faith. Her sweet heat wrapped around him, pulling at every nerve ending on his body, making him crazy with the need to let go. Harder and harder, faster and faster; the mating had gone beyond passion to madness.

Mary clung to his shoulders with a feral intensity, focusing on the building heat between her legs. Her heartbeat pounded against her eardrums, deafening her to everything but the uneven sounds of her own breaths.

In their need to reaffirm their faith in each other, they had taken their fear and desperation and turned it into passion. Using the mind-blowing pleasure of sexual release for an antidote, they had created an emotional fire, and they were burning right down to the bone.

One second Mary was with Daniel stroke for stroke and the next she began to shatter. The rush from the climax all but pulled her off the bed. With an inarticulate cry, she wrapped her legs around Daniel's waist and held him deep inside her. In that instant, his own control finally snapped. A guttural groan ripped up his throat as he spilled himself into her. Still shaking from the adrenaline rush, he collapsed.

"Oh, Daniel…"

"Oh, yeah," he said softly, then pulled her head on his chest and just held her, using her for the anchor that would keep him from complete disintegration.

"Mary…my Mary."

Shuddering slightly as the last convulsions of her climax rippled through her body, Mary lay without moving, savoring Daniel's warmth and strength, as well as the pleasure that only he could give her.

"Go to sleep, darling," Mary whispered.

Daniel was uneasy about letting down his guard, but his trust in Mary Faith was complete, and so he tunneled his hands through her hair and closed his eyes. A short time later he had fallen asleep, his breathing in perfect rhythm to hers.

Howard Lee clocked in at Savannah Memorial Hospital and then proceeded to the basement where the employees' lounge was located. He put his lunch in the refrigerator, along with a sixteen-ounce bottle of pop, then took off his jacket, shaking off the raindrops before hanging it inside his locker. He took out a pair of coveralls and pulled them over his street clothes, then exited the lounge and headed toward the storage room. A few minutes later he had filled his cleaning cart and was ready to begin his shift on the third floor pediatric ward. He had always planned on furthering his education, but taking care of his mother in her waning years had ended most of that. And he'd never been able to channel his loneliness afterward into anything substantial. Now, since he'd embarked upon the quest to create his own family, his lifestyle precluded any long-term commitment to getting a degree. Besides, Howard Lee was of the belief that manual labor was good for the body. His father had been a drywall contractor and he'd grown up watching men make a living by manual skill, as well as physical strength. He did not consider it beneath him to clean floors and toilets, and besides, the job was perfect—low-key and virtually anonymous. He was counting on the fact that the people who push the brooms were all but invisible, and when it was time to move on, he would not be missed.

He moved from room to room on the floor, doing what he'd been hired to do without communicating with anyone else. Only now and then did a nurse address him, and when they did, it was impersonal.

Yesterday he'd overheard two nurses talking and only after he'd listened for a moment, realized they'd been talking about him. They thought he was slow-witted. Retarded, his mother used to say. But he wasn't. He knew because people who were slow-witted couldn't take care of themselves, and he'd been taking care of himself and his mother almost all his life. He started to tell them they were wrong—that he not only took care of himself and his two daughters—but he also drove a car. Then he discarded the notion. He didn't care what they thought.

He picked up a handful of new trash bags and looped them on his belt, then moved into the next room. Only a few more hours, and he could go home to his girls.

Chapter 9

It had been a long night and it was just after 7:00 a.m. when Howard Lee got home. He was tired and in desperate need of sleep, but first, he had to feed his daughters. He reminded himself it was a sacrifice that every good parent must make—tending to their children's needs before tending to their own. In lieu of the hot food he normally served, he filled two bowls with cereal, got cups and spoons from the cabinets, plucked a couple of bananas from a bowl on the sideboard and set it all on a tray, then headed for his room. Kicking aside the throw rug, he set the tray on his bed, lifted the cellar door and called down to the girls.

"Good morning, my darlings...Daddy's home."

He thought nothing of the fact that they didn't answer, but when he got to the bottom of the stairs and realized they were still in bed, he frowned.

"Girls...breakfast. I brought your favorite Crunchy Crispies."

One of them moaned as he set the tray on the table and turned toward the twin beds. He lifted the covers and started to shake them awake.

"Girls...wake up. Breakfast is ready."

Justine whimpered but didn't open her eyes. Amy Anne rolled limply beneath his touch. He frowned. Something wasn't right. They'd never behaved this way before. Then he noticed the bright red flush on their cheeks and laid the back of his hand against Justine's forehead. It was hot to the touch. His heart skipped a beat as he did the same to Amy Anne. She was even hotter. He panicked.

Oh Lord. Oh no.

This hadn't been part of the plan. His babies were sick and taking them to a doctor was out of the question. The authorities would find out that the adoptions weren't final and then they would take them away from him. But what could he do?

Mary woke slowly, coming from a deep, dreamless sleep to total consciousness in tiny increments, remembering the panic of thinking Daniel had disappeared, then finding him standing out in the storm, like a soldier on sentry. She shivered, reliving the abandonment of their lovemaking and remembering that she had barely existed when she'd lost him before. She could hear the shower running in their bathroom and closed her eyes, picturing his big, beautiful body all steamy and wet. Before she could follow up on the thought of joining him, she heard the door to their bedroom open. She rolled over and smiled as Hope peeked inside. Seeing Daniel in the child she'd given birth to made the love she felt for her even more intense.

"Hey, little girl...you're awake awfully early."

"Mommy, can we have waffles?"

Mary grinned. "*May* we have waffles."

Hope's little brows knitted in confusion. "That's what I asked you. I thought you would know."

Mary laughed, and pulled back the covers. "Want to get in bed with me for a while?"

"Am I getting waffles?"

"You bet," Mary said.

"With peanut butter and jelly instead of syrup?"

"If you can eat them like that, I can cook them," Mary promised.

"Goody," Hope said, and crawled in bed with Mary, dragging her one-eared bunny as she went.

"Why don't kids ever sleep late on Saturdays?" Mary muttered, more to herself than to Hope, as she scooted her close to her side.

Hope looked at her mother as if she'd suddenly lost her mind for asking such a dumb question.

"Because we'd miss the best cartoons," she said, and pointed toward the television mounted on the wall. "Can I watch cartoons until Daddy is through taking his bath?"

"If you'll say *may,* and not *can.*"

Hope grinned. "May."

"May what?" Mary asked.

"I don't know," Hope said, then she suddenly smiled. "Oh! I know! May I watch cartoons and may I have waffles! Right, Mommy?"

Mary wrapped her arms around her daughter as she laughed aloud.

"Yes, that's right, sweet pea." She reached for the

remote and turned on the TV, then searched the channels until she found the Disney channel. "Okay. Two cartoons, then down to breakfast, okay?"

Hope nodded, her focus already shifting to the cartoon characters appearing on the screen.

"Hey," Daniel said, as he exited the bathroom in a pair of dilapidated gray sweatpants. "How did I get so lucky as to find my two favorite girls in my bed?"

Before Hope could answer, he pounced, sending her into fits of shrieks and squeals.

Mary escaped, grabbing clothes as she headed for the bathroom. She washed her face and brushed her teeth, dressing quickly before pulling her hair up into a ponytail, shifting her focus from wife to mother with ease, as if she'd done so many times before.

She paused in front of the mirror, giving herself a quick glance before turning away. Her hand was on the doorknob when something made her hesitate. She stood there a moment, staring down at her fingers, absently noting that she'd broken a nail, and then closed her eyes and took a slow deep breath. There was no earthly way she could explain what she suddenly felt or how she knew it—but she knew it just the same. She turned around and faced herself in the mirror, curious to know if she looked any different.

But her appearance was still the same—hair the color of dark caramel that barely brushed her shoulders, bluish-green eyes in a too-slender face, and lips slightly bruised from the passion of last night's lovemaking. And still a little too thin.

But she knew that would change.

She reached toward the mirror, laying the flat of her hand against the glass, then against her belly.

Last night had been magic. She and Daniel had made love—and also a baby.

She shivered suddenly, uncomfortable with the strong feeling of precognition. Even though another child with Daniel would be a true blessing, there was too much going on now to let herself lose focus. Hope's safety had to come first.

A short while later, the first waffle was baking and the sounds of Hope's laughter and Daniel's commentary on the cartoons kept drifting down the stairs. Mary smiled to herself as she got out some plates and began setting the table. As she did, she went over the things that she needed to do. There was an accumulation of Daniel's suits that needed to go to the cleaners, a grocery list that would take at least two hours to complete, and she'd never been happier. All she had to do was think back to the emptiness of her life before to put things in perspective.

"Mommy...is my waffle done yet?"

"Almost," Mary said, as Hope slipped into her seat at the table. "Where's Daddy?"

"Right behind her," Daniel said, as he came in the kitchen and swooped Mary off her feet, then kissed her soundly in front of Hope.

Hope giggled. "Daddy's funny."

"Daddy makes Mommy's toes curl," Mary whispered, careful that only Daniel could hear.

Daniel grinned. "Given another chance...I can do better than that."

"Be still my heart," Mary said, and wiggled her eyebrows.

"Mommy...my waffle!"

Mary spun out of Daniel's arms and headed for the waffle iron.

"One waffle, coming up!"

"With peanut butter and starberry jelly?"

"Of course," Mary said. "Is there any other way?"

"One can only hope," Daniel muttered, and poured himself a cup of coffee before taking his seat.

Mary took the waffle out of the waffle iron and put in on a plate, then began fixing it as Hope had ordered. It wasn't until she was carrying it to the table that she realized her memories were changing. It seemed she'd done this countless times before.

"Yum, Mommy. You always make the best breakfasts," Hope said, and then took her first bite.

"Always?" Mary asked.

"As long as I can remember," Hope mumbled.

As long as she can remember. Mary turned away quickly and began pouring batter into the waffle iron to make another waffle, unwilling for anyone to see that her eyes were filling with tears.

"What's on the agenda, today, honey?" Daniel asked.

"For starters, clothes to the cleaners and groceries."

"Hope and I can take the clothes to the cleaners and pick up some fertilizer for the lawn at the garden center. You make the grocery run and we should all be back home together about the same time. How's that for organization?"

Mary took a deep breath and made herself smile. "It's perfect. Thank you."

Daniel winked at his daughter. "It's our pleasure, isn't it Hope?"

"Yes, we'll help you, Mommy. We're your good helpers, aren't we?"

"You sure are," Mary said. "I don't know what I would do without you...either of you."

She poured a glass of juice for Hope and took it to the table, lingering long enough to smooth her hand down the back of the little girl's hair. Her hands were shaking as she went back to retrieve the next waffle, because she *did* know what it was like to be without them. It's just that they would never understand.

Howard Lee slipped into the lower level of the hospital where he worked and made a beeline for his locker. It was his day off, but no one would know the difference. His job schedule was the last thing of concern in a place where, daily, people fought for their lives. Once in his hospital coveralls with the ID badge clipped to his pocket, he was all but invisible to the staff. He dressed quickly, grabbing a mop bucket and a mop to use as cover in case he was questioned, then headed for the pediatric ward. The main pharmacy for the hospital was on a different floor, but each floor stored a small supply of certain drugs, and he knew where they were kept. All he had to do was create a diversion, take what he needed and no one would be the wiser. He'd heard the staff commenting about a strain of flu going around and decided that was what had made his girls sick. He also remembered enough from his own childhood illnesses to guess what medicines a doctor might prescribe.

Moments later, he exited the elevator on the third floor, pausing a moment to locate the staff on duty, then waited until the hall was empty. Without hesitation, he pulled the fire alarm and then slipped into a laundry closet, well aware that an evacuation would immediately begin. In the confusion, he could get what he needed and be gone before anyone knew what he'd taken. Oh sure, they would eventually miss the drugs, but since he'd clocked out at seven this morning, he would be beyond suspicion.

The sounds of running footsteps sounded in the hallway as nurses began calling out to each other, readying to evacuate their floor. As soon as the footsteps moved away, Howard Lee stuffed his employee ID into his pocket and slipped out of the closet. Two nurses ran past him as he ran toward the drug room behind the nurses' station, but just as he predicted, they paid him no mind. He had to restrain himself from smiling as he slipped behind the desk and then into the room behind.

With little effort, he picked the lock on the drug cabinet, opened the doors, and reached for a bottle of penicillin, when he suddenly remembered the Medic Alert bracelet that Amy Anne wore. She was allergic to penicillin. His mother had been allergic to penicillin. He would have to take a substitute for her. After a quick scan of the shelves, he took two different antibiotics, slipped the vials inside his pocket and relocked the cabinets. On the way out of the room, he grabbed a handful of disposable syringes and headed for the stairwell at the far end of the hallway.

Within minutes, his coveralls were back in his locker and he was leaving through the employees' lounge just as the first of the fire trucks arrived. Fifteen minutes later, he pulled into the driveway of his home, parked in the garage, then dashed into the house. He hurried through the rooms, then down the stairs into the cellar.

Panicked that the girls didn't appear to have moved, he took the antibiotics and two syringes from his pocket, then hurried to their bedside, his heart pounding with fear. At that moment, he realized he hadn't considered the dosages. What if he gave them too much and they died?

Groaning, he dropped onto the mattress at the foot of Amy Anne's bed, his legs too weak to stand. Their breathing was shallow, their faces flushed. He kept thinking that if he did nothing, they would only get worse. They might even die. He was still trying to decide what to do when Justine rolled over on her back and started to cry.

"My head's hot. I want my Mommy. Please, I want my Mommy."

That did it.

Howard Lee set his jaw and took out the first syringe, shook the vial of penicillin because it seemed like a prudent thing to do, and then drew the syringe half-full. He started to pull back the covers and then remembered the area where he administered the shots needed to be disinfected. He grabbed some cotton swabs and a bottle of alcohol from the bathroom then hurried back to the girls. Gritting his teeth, he reached for Justine.

He'd never given anyone a shot before and started to plunge the needle into her tiny arm when he realized he was doing it all wrong. Children's arms were too small. There wasn't enough muscle. It had to go in a hip.

He set the syringe down on the bedside table and pulled down her covers. She whimpered in protest and pushed at his hands as he tugged at the hem of her gown.

"No, no," Howard Lee said. "Daddy is sorry, but he has to do this."

He rubbed the alcohol swab on her backside, took a deep breath and plunged the needle into her flesh, praying that he was doing this right.

The little girl wailed as the antibiotic went in—a high-pitched, feverish squeal that tore at his conscience. He told himself her shriek was from the shock of the needle prick and not an overdose of medicine, but he couldn't be sure until some time had passed.

Still shaking, he withdrew the used syringe and laid it aside, got out a fresh one, drew a dose from the other vial for Amy Anne and gave her an injection, too. The fact that she didn't even acknowledge the pain, was, to Howard Lee, even more frightening.

Once the medicine had been given, he got a washcloth and a basin of cool water and proceeded to bathe their arms and faces. Afterward, he put them in fresh nightgowns and then sat beside their beds, watching until they fell back asleep.

Convinced that he'd done all he knew to do, he gathered up the uneaten food and medicine and went upstairs. As always, he closed the cellar door and locked it behind him, but for the first time since he'd "adopted" the girls, he felt guilt.

He'd gone to great lengths to make sure that their room had been well-lit and ventilated, and that they had plenty of toys and games to entertain them, but it was still a cellar all the same. And, no matter how many ways he tried to justify it, there was nothing healthy about raising children below ground. In his single-minded intent to acquire a family, he'd thought more of himself than the children. He should have provided different accommodations—certainly safer ones. But that was hindsight. He had to deal with the ramifications of what he'd done and then make it better.

He put the antibiotics into the refrigerator then dumped the uneaten food into the garbage disposal. Although his body was crying out for sleep, there were too many things to be done before he could let himself rest, the first of which was to buy food that would be more enticing for sick children.

He popped a couple of No-Sleeps into his mouth and washed them down with a glass of milk, then started to make a grocery list. The first item he wrote down was soup. As a child, it was what his mother had fed him, and his mother had always done what was right.

He finished the list, then went to check on the girls one last time before leaving the house. They seemed to be resting a little easier. Satisfied that he had done the right thing, he hurried back up the stairs and out the door to the supermarket.

Reese Arnaud sat at his desk, staring at the sketch of the blond-headed man with funny teeth. It had gone out last night with the late shift of officers and even though he'd known it would be a long shot, he'd hoped for some news this morning when he'd come to work.

But when he'd reached his desk and found nothing but a handful of phone messages regarding other cases, his hopes had been dashed. Disappointed, he reached for his coffee cup. Phone time was prime time for sneaking that extra jolt of caffeine, and something told him he was going to need it today.

A short while later, he had returned all the calls and was finishing up some paperwork when his gaze fell on the sketch once again. He picked it up, then cursed softly beneath his breath. The more he looked at it, the more he realized what a stretch this was going to be. Just because some man got too friendly with one little girl on public school grounds did not mean he was the person responsible for the disappearance of two others. The world was full of perverts. Assuming that this one was the one they were looking for was too much to expect.

A muscle jerked at the side of his jaw and he could feel another pulling at the corner of his eyelid. They needed a break in this case—and soon. He had to find those missing girls. Maybe then he would be able to sleep.

Mary stood at the door waving goodbye to Daniel and Hope, then hurried back into the house to get her purse. Daniel had promised Hope a trip to the park this afternoon and Mary wanted to go, too. Being given a second chance had made her all too aware of how precious life was and how swiftly it could be taken away.

As she swung her purse over her shoulder, something bumped against her side. Frowning, she thrust her hand into the bag. Moments later, her fingers curled around her cell phone. Her purse was already heavy and she started to leave it behind, then at the last second, changed her mind. With one last glance around the room, she hurried out the door, taking care to lock it behind her. A short while later she was pulling into the supermarket parking lot with nothing more serious on her mind than what kind of breakfast cereal to buy.

Howard Lee was standing in the soup aisle, debating with himself as to whether it would be more judicious to purchase dehydrated soup that came pre-packed in envelopes or the canned kinds that only needed to be heated. He wished his mother was still alive. She would know which kinds of soups sick children preferred.

A woman with two toddlers at her heels turned down the aisle in which he was standing. He watched her coming and considered asking her for advice, but her children were raising such a fuss he decided against it. He winced at the shrillness in her voice as she yelled at one of the kids to shut up. It was a good thing he'd decided against talking to her. She wouldn't have anything positive to say.

Frustrated, he picked up a can of chicken noodle soup and began reading the instructions. Heat and eat seemed simple enough. Maybe that would work. He tossed a half-dozen cans in his shopping cart and then moved slowly down the aisles, adding a box of crackers, a couple of jars of flavored applesauce and a small bag of vanilla wafers.

He was on his way to the checkout counter when he remembered he was almost out of milk and juice. Wheeling the cart in a quick one-eighty, he found himself face-to-face with a pretty dark-haired woman who was just turning down the aisle. Their carts bumped slightly and then each of them swerved in an opposite direction.

"Oh! Excuse me!" Howard Lee said, and then

smiled bashfully. "These things need horns and sirens on them, don't they?"

Mary started to apologize for her own inattention to what she'd been doing and then she focused on his smile. She knew he was waiting for a response from her, but she couldn't speak for staring at the spaces between his teeth.

"Ma'am...are you all right?" Howard Lee asked, thinking he must have bumped her harder than he'd first believed.

Mary blinked. "Uh...yes...I'm fine." She took a deep breath, trying to calm a racing heart as her gaze slid to his face. A tall skinny man with yellow hair, round eyes and funny teeth. A clown face. Just like Hope had described.

Howard Lee frowned. What was wrong with this woman? Then he looked at her again, thinking she looked vaguely familiar, but he couldn't place where he'd seen her. Shrugging it off, he gripped the shopping cart.

"I'll just be going then," he said. "I need to get home to my girls. They're not feeling too well."

He steered his cart around Mary and moved toward the far end of the store where the refrigerated section was located.

Mary's heart was pounding erratically as she thrust her hand in her purse, searching for the cell phone. She pulled it out with a jerk, then punched in the numbers to Daniel's office with trembling fingers. Twice she messed up and had to start all over. By the time she got the right numbers entered, she was shaking all over.

She closed her eyes as she counted the rings, praying that he would answer.

Howard Lee had the milk in his cart and was reaching for the orange juice when he remembered where he'd seen the woman—at the school—picking up the little girl he was going to adopt. But she hadn't seen him, so it didn't make sense why she would have been staring at him in that way.

He put the orange juice in his cart and then started toward the checkout stand, when he caught sight of her again. She was still in the same aisle, and using her cell phone. That, in itself, didn't set off any alarms until she looked up and saw him watching her. The fear on her face was shocking. In that moment, he knew it was over. He didn't know how it had happened, but he knew that she knew.

The phone was still ringing and Mary was trying to figure out where Daniel had gone and why he didn't answer when she looked up and saw the clown man watching her from the end of the aisle.

"Oh God, oh God," she muttered, debating with herself as to what to do. Then it hit her. Reese. She should be calling Reese Arnaud, not Daniel. She disconnected her call and quickly punched in 9-1-1.

"Savannah P.D., what is your emergency?"

"This is Mary O'Rourke. I'm in Vinter's supermarket and I need you to tell Detective Reese Arnaud that the man he's looking for is here."

"Ma'am…are you in danger?"

"No, I don't think so," Mary mumbled, and then glanced over her shoulder. The man had disappeared. "Oh no," she muttered.

"Ma'am?"

"He's gone," Mary cried. She abandoned her cart in the middle of the aisle and started running toward the front of the store. If he got out of the store before the police arrived, there would be no way of telling which direction he'd gone.

"Who's gone, ma'am?"

"The man! The man!" Mary muttered, resisting the urge to scream. "Just tell Reese Arnaud! Please! He'll know who I mean."

"Yes, ma'am, your message is being relayed at this moment, but I need you to stay on the line."

"Yes, yes, I'm still here," Mary said, puffing slightly as she bolted through the checkout line and out the front door, the phone still pressed to her ear.

She paused in front of the store, searching the parking lot with a frantic gaze, unaware that Howard Lee was watching her from behind the corner of his van.

He'd tossed the groceries into his vehicle and was debating with himself about driving away when he'd seen the woman come running out of the store with the phone still in her hand. At that point, he'd known his suspicions were correct. His first urge was to escape, but he couldn't risk leaving her there. The way she kept looking around the parking lot made him think she was waiting for the police, and that left him no choice.

He jumped in his van and quickly backed out of the parking space, then circled the lot and headed for the front of the store. The woman was still there, the phone clutched to her ear. Knowing the tinted windows in the van would conceal his identity right up to the moment he opened the door, he drove straight for her.

Mary was frantic, certain that she'd lost sight of him for good.

"Please," she begged of the dispatcher. "Did you tell Detective Arnaud? If they don't hurry, it's going to be too late."

"Yes, ma'am, he got the message," the dispatcher said. "The police are on the way. Just stay where you are until they arrive, okay?"

Frustrated, Mary moved a little farther away from the front of the store, still searching for sight of a tall blond man between the parked cars. A white van was coming toward her, then slowing down in front of the loading zone, and she took a couple of steps backward to get out of the way. The van stopped in front of her. She heard the driver's side door open, then heard the footsteps of the driver circling the van.

Before she could react, she was face-to-face with the man she'd been seeking. She threw up her hands and started to run, when he grabbed her by the arm.

"No!" She screamed. "Help! Somebody help me!"

She clawed at his arm, trying to pull herself free. One moment she was screaming bloody murder and then everything went black as he hit her with his fist. She hit the pavement with her elbow, then her chin, but never felt the pain. Seconds later, he dragged her off the street, flung her into the van and sped away.

Her phone was on the pavement beside her purse as the clerk who'd witnessed the event came running

out of the store. She picked up the phone as the
9-1-1 dispatcher kept asking if something was wrong.

"Yes!" the clerk cried. "The woman you were
talking to has just been abducted by a man in a white
van. Please hurry. They're getting away."

Chapter 10

Daniel pulled up in front of the house and parked in the shade of the portico, then glanced in the back seat. Hope was still asleep. Opening the door quietly, he unlocked the house and then went back to the car to carry her inside. She roused briefly.

"Daddy, are we home?"

"Yes, honey, we're home."

"I want bunny," she muttered, without opening her eyes.

"He can take a nap with you, okay?"

She nodded once without bothering to answer.

He smiled as he carried her up the stairs, then down the hall to her room. He pushed the door inward with the toe of his shoe and then laid her on her bed, tucking the one-eared bunny beneath her arm and a blanket over her legs.

She fidgeted briefly, then settled.

Daniel watched until he was sure she was still

sound asleep, then hurried back down the stairs to unload the car. He was just coming out of the house as Reese Arnaud pulled in behind him. He waved and smiled as he opened the trunk of the car, but Reese didn't smile back. A warning bell went off in the back of Daniel's mind, but it wasn't enough to prepare him for the news Arnaud brought.

"What's wrong?"

Reese sighed. It was days like these that made him wish he'd become a priest like his mother had wanted, instead of following his father's footsteps into law enforcement.

"It's Mary," Reese said. "She's been abducted."

Shock, coupled with a mind-blowing pain, ricocheted through Daniel's mind. He took an unsteady step backward and pointed at Reese.

"No, you're wrong. She's just gone to the supermarket. She'll be right back. Come in and I'll make us some coffee until—"

Reese grabbed Daniel, almost shaking him to make him listen.

"She was on the phone to 9-1-1 when it happened. She said she saw the man we're looking for in the market. I don't know exactly what happened, but he must have overheard her in some way and panicked."

Daniel moaned, then staggered backward against his car.

"No…God, no…not Mary. You've got to be mistaken."

"It's not a mistake," Reese said. "I wish to God it was, but we had an eyewitness. A clerk saw it happening. By the time she got outside, they were gone. We know it was a white van. We've got the first three letters on the license plate and a description on the man that fits the one Hope gave us.''

"Why in hell is this happening?"

"If I had to guess, I'd say this is the man who snatched the two little girls.''

"But why take Mary?''

"Who knows? But something put him on the alert and he took her, maybe believing she was the only person who could identify him.''

Daniel paled. "If that's what he thinks, he'll kill her.''

Reese's gut knotted. "I don't know what he's thinking. But he doesn't know about the sketch.''

Daniel grabbed Reese's arm. "You've got to release it now! If the media gets hold of it, he'll realize she's not the only witness. Then he won't think he has to kill her.''

"Already got it covered,'' Reese said. "It went out about a half hour ago, the moment we learned about Mary. We won't take chances with her life, even if it means the man might run.''

Daniel's vision blurred. "This can't be happening.''

"I'm sorry...so sorry,'' Reese said.

Daniel stood for a moment, his head down. Reese thought he was crying, then Daniel looked up.

"If he hurts her, I'll kill him.''

Reese empathized with Daniel, but as a cop, he had to persuade him otherwise.

"You can't think like that. You have a daughter to raise.''

Daniel poked a finger in Reese's chest, his voice so low that Reese had to lean forward to hear.

"You heard me. If he so much as makes her cry,

he'll pray to die before I'm through." Then he turned away and strode toward the house.

"Where are you going?"

"To call my parents to come get Hope, then I'm going to look for my wife."

"Damn it, O'Rourke, you're a lawyer. You know better than this. You've got to leave this to the police."

"Then you better find him before I do," Daniel said, and slammed the door in Reese's face.

Mary woke up in a strange bed and in pain. Her face throbbed where the man had hit her with his fist and her right shoulder and hip were stiff and aching. As she rolled from the bed to her feet, sheer terror hit her like a fist to the gut. The man was here—staring at her from across the room. She didn't know how long he'd been there, or what he'd done to her while she'd been unconscious, but the look in his eyes made her want to throw up.

"Who are you?"

"My name is Howard Lee Martin."

"Okay, Howard Lee...I need to know why you are doing this."

He smiled. It made Mary's skin crawl.

"It's all going to work out for the best, you know."

Mary shuddered. The calm, conversational tone of his voice seemed obscene in the face of what he'd just done.

"What's best is that you let me go home to my family."

His smile turned downward. "This is your family.

You are home now. You'll soon get used to it. I have
a good job and I can take good care of all of us.''

Mary stifled her shock. It wasn't enough that the
man was a criminal, but he had to be crazy, as well.
She wanted to cry—to wail aloud at the injustice of
being snatched from a family she'd just regained, but
something told her that Howard Lee wouldn't deal
well with panic.

"Look, Mr. Martin, I—"

"Not Mr. Martin. Call me Howard Lee and you're
going to be Sophie. It was my mother's name. I loved
my mother deeply. She would be proud to know you
had the same name."

Mary shivered. "My name is Mary, not Sophie. I
can't be a mother to your children because I'm already someone else's mother. I have a daughter,
Howard Lee. She'll be worried about me."

"I have two daughters and they need a mother,
too." Then he pointed over Mary's shoulder. "They
haven't been feeling well. See for yourself. They
need you far more than your child does. Their medicine is on the table. I've already given them injec-
tions for today, but they need to be bathed and fed.
I'll leave you to it."

Mary gasped, then turned. For the first time since
she'd awakened, she saw another small bed pushed
up against the wall. A loud clunk startled her and she
spun back around to find the man had disappeared
and the door he'd come through was closed. She ran
up the steps, screaming for him to come back and let
her out, but the door was heavy and obviously locked
from above. No matter how hard she pushed, it
wouldn't give. Daniel and Hope were bound to be

home from their errands by now. When she didn't come home they would be frantic.

She ran her fingers along the edges, trying to find a weakness in the door, to find a way to set herself free, but the man had been too thorough. She felt nothing but cold, smooth steel.

"No," she muttered, then pounded on the door. "No, no, you can't do this! Let me out! Let me out! Somebody help!"

"No one ever comes but him."

At the sound of the voice, Mary spun. The little girl looking up at her from the foot of the stairs resembled Hope so much that it gave her chills. Thinking how close Hope had come to falling into this awful man's grasp, she took a deep breath and then went back down the steps. If this had to happen, thank God it happened to her and not her baby. She dropped to her knees and then lifted a wayward strand of hair from the little girl's eyes.

"Honey…is he your father?"

The little girl frowned. "No. My daddy's nice."

Oh God…oh God. "Do you know long have you been here?"

"I don't know. Lots of nights, I guess."

Mary shuddered, trying to imagine what those nights had been like.

"What's your name?"

"Justine." She pointed toward the bed. "She's Amy Anne, but she doesn't talk."

Mary stifled a gasp. The two missing girls! My God! They were alive after all. She touched a hand to Justine's forehead. It was hot and dry.

"He said you were sick."

She nodded, then her lower lip quivered and she started to cry.

"I want my Mommy."

"I know, baby," Mary said softly, then picked her up and carried her back to the bed.

She lay Justine down, then smoothed the dark tangles away from her feverish face before turning to the other little girl. She lay on the side of the bed next to the wall, her gaze focused on a spot on the ceiling above her head. When Mary touched her face to test for fever, she didn't even blink.

"Amy Anne…is that your name?"

"She won't talk to you. She doesn't talk to anyone," Justine said, and then coughed.

The cough was more like a rattle deep in the little girl's chest. There was a box of tissues, as well as some cough drops and cough syrup on the table beside the bed. Mary reached for the bottle.

"How about we take a little cough medicine?" Mary asked. "It's grape flavored. Do you like grape?"

Justine nodded, then sat up in bed as Mary poured a measure of the medicine into a small plastic cup.

Justine drank it without comment and Mary wondered what else she had endured without complaint.

"Amy Anne has a cough, too." Justine said.

"Then we'll give her some, too," Mary said. "Okay?"

The child nodded, watching intently as Mary slipped an arm beneath the girl's shoulders and lifted her up.

"Swallow it, honey," Mary urged.

Amy Anne opened her mouth and swallowed. When Mary slid her arm out from under her shoulders, she looked so tiny and lost against the bed-clothes that it broke Mary's heart.

"Come here, babies...it's going to be okay," Mary said, and then crawled into the bed, took both children into her arms and pulled them close. "I'm here. I won't let him hurt you anymore."

"I want to go home," Justine whispered.

"So do I, sweet baby," Mary said. "So do I."

Mike and Phyllis O'Rourke were doing their best to hide the horror of Mary's abduction from their granddaughter. At Daniel's bidding, they were taking her home to spend the weekend, and Hope was so excited she hadn't realized Mary was not back from the supermarket. It wasn't until she was packed and ready to leave that she mentioned her mother.

"Daddy, I didn't get to tell Mommy goodbye."

Daniel was struggling with tears as he picked Hope up and held her to his chest.

"I'll tell her for you, okay?" he said, as he kissed her cheek.

Hope smiled. "Okay. And give her this, too." She blew a kiss in her own hand and then handed it to Daniel as if it was real.

Daniel pretended to take it and put it in his pocket, then hugged her again before setting her down.

"Mommy's going to love that," he said. "I'll be sure she gets it." He looked at his parents, who were struggling to keep smiles on their own faces, too. "I'll call," he promised.

Mike nodded, while Phyllis didn't trust herself to speak. Instead, she picked up Hope's overnight bag, then took Hope by the hand.

"We'll be in the car," she said.

Mike stayed behind, not knowing what to say, but aware that his son was at a breaking point.

"Daniel...I'm so sorry. I don't know what to say to make this better."

"There's nothing to say."

"Please don't do anything rash. Let the police do their job."

A muscle jerked in Daniel's jaw. "What if this had happened to Mom?"

Mike sighed. "Just remember you've still got a daughter to raise."

"She deserves both parents, Dad, not just me."

"Just be careful," Mike cautioned.

"There's no time for caution. I've got to find her, or life won't be worth living."

"Not even for Hope?"

"No Dad...because of Hope. She needs Mary as much or more than I do. I don't know how long this is going to take, but I thank you and Mom for taking care of her."

Tears welled in Mike's eyes. "No thanks are necessary. Just stay in touch."

Daniel walked his father to the door, then stood on the doorstep and waved until they were gone. The moment he was alone, he went back in the house and headed for his office. He couldn't let himself think about what Mary was going through or he'd lose it completely, but waiting helplessly while someone else went to rescue his reason for living made no sense. Arnaud said the man who took her was the same man that Hope had seen. That couldn't be good. He had to know he'd been made. It also meant that Mary's life was, more than likely, hanging on a very thin thread. He took a deep breath and then swiped his hands across his face.

"Ah God...please...don't take her away from me."

Before he could think past the prayer, the phone rang. He grabbed it immediately, needing it to be Mary.

"Hello."

"Mr. Daniel O'Rourke?"

His heart started to hammer. "Yes, this is Daniel O'Rourke."

"Mr. O'Rourke, how much do you pay for your long distance service?"

Daniel stared at the phone in disbelief and then slammed the receiver down on the cradle. Seconds later, he picked up the paperweight and flung it angrily toward the fireplace. It hit the brick firewall with a vicious thud then shattered in a dozen pieces.

"Damn, damn, damn it all to hell!"

He'd talked big to Reese Arnaud, but the truth was he didn't have the first idea of how to start looking for Mary Faith.

He slumped against the desk, his gaze wandering aimlessly about the room as he waited for a miracle. He sat that way for several minutes, unmoving— mind blank to everything but the panic threatening to overwhelm him.

It was a bit before he began to realize that he was staring at a small framed picture hanging on the wall. When he finally focused on what he'd been looking at, he reached for the phone. It would take more than a miracle to find Mary Faith. He needed help, and from someone who had no qualms about bending the law.

* * *

Bobby Joe Killian tossed his gun and holster on his desk, then sat down in his chair and kicked back with a weary groan. His head hurt, and he would give half a month's wages for a thick steak and a good massage.

The sign on the door to his office read Killian Investigations, but he considered it more than slightly deceiving. The last three cases he'd been on had been more like hunts. Hunting for cheating wives and men who'd jumped bail. The money was good—damned good—but the lifestyle was getting harder and harder to keep up with.

He glanced at his watch and then picked up the phone. It said something for his personal life that the first number on his automatic dial was his bookie.

"Harrison, this is Bobby Joe. Give me five hundred on Merlin's Pride in the fifth."

"Damn it, Bobby Joe. You still owe me for the last race you bet on. What makes you think I'm stupid enough to do this again?"

Bobby Joe grinned as he pivoted his chair toward the windows. The view from his third-floor office was not exactly on the tourist route, but it suited his purposes. Being low-profile was invaluable. The less his face was known, the better he was able to do his job. He thrust his fingers through his dark, too-long hair, absently combing it away from his face, then reached for a couple of peanuts from a dish on his desk and began shelling them onto the floor as he continued to talk.

"Now Harrison, you know damn good and well you still owe me for that last bail-jumper I found for you. The way I see it, I've still got a good fifteen hundred dollars in credit and I'm spending a nickel of it today.''

A string of muffled curses rolled through the line and into Bobby Joe's ears. He grinned to himself and popped the peanuts into his mouth as the bookie continued to vent.

''Hey, Harrison...you about finished?''

''Does it really matter?'' the bookie muttered.

''Sure it does,'' Bobby Joe said. ''You know I care what you think.''

''Bull.''

''So...are we still on the same page?''

''Oh, hell yes, I've got the whole book in my lap. Is that what you wanted to hear?''

''It'll do,'' Bobby Joe said, and then cut the man short when his phone started beeping in his ear. ''Got another call. Make my bet.''

He hit the flash button and then answered again.

''Killian Investigations.''

''Bobby Joe, I need your help.''

Bobby Joe's feet hit the floor, inadvertently crushing peanut hulls beneath his boots.

''Daniel?''

''Yeah, it's me.''

''What's wrong?''

''Mary's been abducted.''

''Abducted? My God!''

''Help me,'' Daniel said.

''Are you home?''

''Yes.''

''I'm on my way.''

Howard Lee snored in his sleep. The sound roused him just enough that he rolled from his back to his side. A few seconds later, his arm slid off the bed, his fingers dangling toward the floor only inches from the cellar door. He shifted slightly then settled, confident that his family was close by. His alarm was set for 4:00 p.m. It would give him plenty of time to get some rest before preparing his family's supper. His girls would be fine now that he'd brought the woman. Little Justine had been right. Sick children need a mother. He sighed, then licked his lips before falling back into a deep, dreamless sleep.

Mary was afraid to close her eyes. Just the thought of that man coming back and finding her sleeping and vulnerable made her sick to her stomach. Both little girls still lay in her arms, although the fever she'd felt on their bodies earlier seemed to be subsiding.

Even in her sleep, Justine clung to Mary in quiet desperation, her fingers wrapped in the fabric of her clothes. The other child, the one Justine called Amy Anne, was too still. Mary could only imagine the horror that she had gone through, being the first child taken—being put into this place all alone—having to suffer through whatever hell the man had put her through. She wondered how long she had endured before she'd slipped this far away. A child who couldn't cry was a child too close to death.

Mary pulled her closer, holding her gently against her breast. She needed to do something to try and bring Amy Anne back from the mental precipice on which she was hovering, but wasn't certain what would be safe. The last thing she wanted to do was drive her even farther away from reality, so she started to talk, unwilling to give Amy Anne permission to slip any farther away.

"Amy Anne, my name is Mary. I know you're afraid. We're all afraid, but we're going to be all right. People are looking for us. Did you know that? Oh, yes, it's true. And you know what else? I have a little girl who's just about your age. Her name is Hope. When we get out of here and go home, maybe you and Justine can come to my house and play with her. She would like that, and so would I."

Mary swallowed, fighting back tears. *Daniel...I need you. Please find me.*

Justine shifted on the bed beside her and then opened her eyes. Mary looked down at her and smiled.

"You're still here," the little girl said.

Mary nodded.

Justine sighed. "I thought I'd dreamed you."

"No, baby. It's not a dream." *It's a nightmare.* "I'm right beside you."

Justine sniffed and looked at Amy Anne. "Is she going to talk to us?"

Mary's gaze shifted back to the child in her arms. Her face was pale and immobile, as was her body. If she hadn't felt her warmth, she would have thought she was dead.

"I don't know. I hope so. Did she ever talk to you?"

"No."

"Not even when you were first here?"

"Nope. Not even when I used to cry."

"You don't cry anymore?"

Justine shrugged. "Sometimes...but not so he can see me. It makes him mad when I cry."

Mary shivered. This was hell and he was the devil. "Does he hurt you?"

"No."

Mary hesitated, almost afraid to ask anything more, but she needed to know what was in store. She had to be prepared for the worst, should it come.

"Does he do other things to you, honey? Does he touch you in places he shouldn't?"

Justine frowned. "He brings us food and brushes our hair. We always fall asleep after supper."

"You mean, after you've bathed and put on your nightgowns?"

Justine shook her head. "Oh no. I don't remember taking baths except I know I'm always clean because I smell good. And I don't put on my own nightgown. The man does it, I guess. I don't remember."

Mary's flesh crawled. *Dear God, he must be doping their food. God only knows what happens after that.*

Chapter 11

Bobby Joe Killian came to a sliding halt in Daniel's driveway. Seconds later, the police cruiser that had been in pursuit pulled in behind him. He got out holding his ID and walked toward the patrolman who was emerging from the car with his gun in his hand.

"Hey, Doolan, is that you?" Bobby Joe asked.

Officer Henry Doolan recognized the drawl behind the too-long hair, then rolled his eyes and holstered his gun.

"Thunderation, Killian, a man driving like a bat out of hell...I should have known it was you." Then he gestured toward the low-slung sports car Bobby Joe was driving. "When did you get that?"

"Last month. Won it in a poker game."

"You ran a stop sign," Doolan growled.

Bobby Joe gestured toward the house. "Sorry. I was in a hurry. Official business."

Doolan snorted. "Oh yeah, right. You expect me to believe that?"

"It's true," Bobby Joe said. "Daniel O'Rourke lives here. His wife has been abducted."

Doolan's smirk disappeared. "The woman from Vinter's supermarket?"

"I don't know where it happened. All I know is a friend called for help and I came. You gonna give me a ticket or what? I've got a good woman to go find."

Doolan cursed beneath his breath and then pointed a finger in Bobby Joe's face.

"You lucked out this time, Killian. Under the circumstances, I'll let this slide. But next time, pay the hell attention, will you?"

"You got it, Doolan, and thanks," Bobby Joe said, and headed for the front door.

Before he could knock, Daniel jerked it open, then saw the police car pulling away.

"I'm not going to ask what that was about," Daniel said.

"It was nothing," Bobby Joe said. "Tell me about Mary."

Daniel's expression never changed, although Bobby Joe could tell he was in shock.

"She's gone."

Bobby Joe pushed his way past Daniel and walked into the house.

"We'll get her back, buddy. Now tell me everything you know."

Howard Lee woke up slowly, trying to remember what was different in his home and then he smiled as he stretched and kicked back the covers. He'd brought a mother home for the girls. He hadn't planned on doing it so suddenly, but considering what had transpired, he'd had no choice.

Reluctantly, he made himself get up. Swinging his legs over the side of the bed, he felt the cool metal of the cellar door beneath his feet, thought of her— his very own Sophie, and smiled.

Mary was sitting cross-legged on the bed with Amy Anne in her lap and Justine scrunched up beside her. A couple of hours ago Justine had awakened and headed straight for the television. Mary knew this must be part of her normal routine and marveled at the resiliency of youth. Personally, she would like to give in to her fear and frustration and scream bloody murder. Before she could follow the thought, she heard something squeak, then a solid thump followed. She bolted from the bed and started toward the stairs when suddenly Howard Lee was there, coming down the steps carrying a tray full of food. She stopped in midstep and then began backing up.

"Sophie...darling!" Howard Lee said. "What a warm welcome! I couldn't ask for anything more."

Ignoring the fact that he was calling her by another name, Mary pleaded with him.

"Mr....please, let us go."

"Howard Lee. You must call me Howard Lee."

The smile on his face was too broad. The look in his eyes too full of an expectation she could never fulfill.

"The girls are sick. Please let me take them to a doctor."

He put the tray down on the table and then began to set the places, just as he did at every meal. Ignoring her request, he looked at the girls and gestured toward the food.

"Sit down," he said shortly.

Justine quickly did as he asked, but Mary stayed where she was.

Howard Lee looked at the girls and then frowned at Mary.

"Sophie! They're still in their nightgowns. As their mother, I expected you to at least brush their hair and help them dress. I can't do everything by myself forever. I have a job, you know."

Great...he's not just a pervert...he's crazy, too.

Even though she was afraid, she held her ground.

"They've been in bed all day and are more comfortable in their gowns."

Howard Lee's frown deepened. "I don't want them to appear slovenly."

"Then get them out of this cellar and into the sunshine," Mary snapped.

Howard Lee spun angrily. Suddenly the spoon in his hand took on an ominous appearance.

"You don't talk to me like that," he snapped. "A wife is supposed to honor her husband."

"I do honor my husband," Mary said. "His name is Daniel."

Howard Lee hit her with the flat of his hand. The sound echoed in the sudden silence of the room.

Mary groaned. It was the same place he'd hit her before and the ache went all the way to the back of her teeth. He hovered over her as he glared, but she wouldn't let him see her fear.

"So you're into hitting women as well as stealing other people's children. I wonder what other ugly little secrets you're hiding."

Rage rolled through Howard Lee like tide on the shore, ebbing and flowing in sudden surges. She was talking back to him. How dare she talk back? Didn't she know what a terrible example she was setting for the girls?

"You don't talk to me like that in front of our girls."

Mary doubled up her fists and laughed. It was an ugly, choking sound that was too close to a sob, but she couldn't take it back. It was too late and her rage was too swift.

"Those aren't our girls. They belong to four other people who are desperate to get them back. I don't know why you're doing this but I can tell you it's never going to work."

Howard Lee grabbed her arm and yanked her hard against his chest.

"It's already working," he said. "They're my girls. Do you hear me? I adopted them. The papers will be coming through any day now and then you'll see."

There was coffee on his breath and a fleck of spittle at the corner of his mouth and Mary felt like throwing up.

"What about me?" she asked. "There aren't any papers, real or imagined, that are going to make kidnapping me okay. The police might stop looking for us, but my husband never will."

"Don't threaten me," Howard Lee growled. "I can make you disappear."

Mary's heart sank. It was nothing more than what she'd feared all along, but she'd be damned if she'd let him know it mattered.

"It won't matter how many times you kill me,

Howard Lee. He knows what you look like. The police know what you look like, too. You can't hide forever.''

Howard Lee paled.

"You're lying."

Mary shrugged. "Believe what you want."

Howard Lee shoved the rest of the food from the tray and stomped up the stairs, dropping the door shut with a resounding thud. Mary flinched at the sound, but by God, she'd stood her ground.

"You made him mad," Justine said.

Mary turned and looked down at the little girl, then grinned.

"I did, didn't I?"

Justine hesitated just a moment and then slipped her hand in Mary's hand and smiled.

Mary winked at her. "I told you it was going to be okay, didn't I?"

Justine pointed at Amy Anne.

"You have to hold her on your lap to help her eat."

Mary nodded. "Okay. Thank you, Justine."

"You're welcome."

Mary went to the bed and picked up the little girl, then sat down at the table with Amy Anne in her lap.

"Hey, kiddo. How about some supper? Looks like we've got chicken noodle soup and cheese sandwiches. Do you like chicken noodle soup? I do. Ooh, and I see chocolate chip cookies for dessert. How about a cookie, Amy Anne?"

She put the cookie in Amy Anne's fingers, then scooped up a spoonful of soup and held it to the little girl's mouth. Amy Anne's lips opened like a baby bird and Mary slipped the soup inside.

Justine looked at the cookie Amy Anne was holding.

"We're not supposed to eat dessert first," she said.

"I know," Mary said. "But this place is different, isn't it? The man broke the rules first, so we can too."

Justine thought about it a moment and then giggled.

Mary wanted to cry. It was the first time she'd seen her really smile.

"Is your soup too hot?"

"Nope. It's just right," Justine said.

"Then eat it up before it gets cold, okay?"

"Okay."

Mary took a bite of her own cheese sandwich and then spooned another bite of soup into Amy Anne's mouth. She was reaching for her juice when she remembered that Howard Lee was doping them with sedatives. She set Amy Anne aside and then picked up the glasses and took them to the bathroom, poured out the juice, and filled the glasses with water. As she walked back to the table, she saw Amy Anne lift the cookie to her mouth and take a bite.

Justine gasped. "Look, Mary! Look at Amy Anne! She's feeding herself."

"Is that good?"

"I think so," Justine said. "I've never seen her do it before."

Mary set the water glasses down and gave Amy Anne a quick hug.

"I'll bet she can do lots of things, can't you honey?"

Mary felt the momentary weight of the little girl's

body against her, as if she'd leaned into the hug, and then the moment was gone.

"You're going to be just fine, little girl," Mary said softly, and pressed a kiss against her cheek. "Now let's eat our supper. Afterward we can play some games or maybe work some puzzles. Do you like to play puzzles?"

Amy Anne didn't answer, but it didn't matter. She was eating on her own.

Daniel stood on the sidewalk in front of Vinter's supermarket, staring down at the pavement where several small specks of blood had been circled with chalk. The area had been roped off with yellow crime scene tape and all of the videotapes from the supermarket's security cameras had been confiscated by the police. While Bobby Joe didn't have access to the tapes, he was working his magic on the clerk who'd witnessed the abduction. Between the flashing smile and his dark, bad-boy looks, Bobby Joe Killian could get just about anything he wanted.

And according to the clerk, this was where Mary had been taken. The man had hit her with his fist and shoved her into a late model white van. They had the first three letters of the license tag and a description of the man that fit the one Hope had given them, but no idea of where to look first.

Daniel spun away from the blood-spattered sidewalk and looked back into the store where Bobby Joe had gone. He could see him through the window, still talking to the clerk. Daniel doubled up his fists and strode toward the car. He'd never felt this helpless or this afraid. He couldn't let himself think of what Mary must be enduring, or if she was even alive. He sat down inside Bobby Joe's sports car and waited for him to return.

Less than five minutes later, Bobby Joe came out of the store on the run. When he slid behind the wheel, he was grinning.

"Tell me something to make me smile, too," Daniel said.

Bobby Joe started the car and put it in gear, peeling out of the parking lot.

"Do we know where we're going?"

Bobby Joe looked at Daniel and then grinned.

"Hell yes. We're going to find Mary Faith."

Daniel wished he felt as optimistic as Bobby Joe acted.

"What did the clerk tell you that she didn't tell the police?"

Bobby Joe looked at him and then grinned.

"She said the guy is a regular, that he shops in there at least once a week, and for the past few weeks has been buying the same kind of stuff that parents with small kids usually buy."

"How does that help us?"

"If he's recently started buying food geared toward kids, then we can assume he's got some kids to feed. And...if he shops in there on a regular basis, then he must live in the area. I've got a friend in the department of motor vehicles running down the license numbers. Once we get a printout, we can compare it to the addresses in the area. It's all a matter of elimination."

"How long will that take?" Daniel asked.

"I don't know...maybe first thing tomorrow."

Daniel groaned and hit the dashboard with the flat of his hand. "Damn...damn...damn."

"What?" Bobby Joe asked.

"All night…in that man's grasp? I can't let that happen."

Bobby Joe shook his head. "I know, Daniel. I wish to hell I had a better answer."

"It's not knowing that makes it so bad."

"Knowing what?"

Daniel didn't answer and Bobby Joe knew he was hurting bad.

"Talk to me, friend."

Daniel shuddered and had to swallow twice before he could spit out the words.

"What he's doing to her. I don't know what he's doing to her. I imagine the worst. Every minute I breathe without knowing where she is is like a knife in my heart."

Bobby Joe sighed. "We'll find her, Daniel."

"We have to."

"Yeah, I know."

But he didn't. He had no ties to anyone in the way that Daniel and Mary felt about each other, and it was just the way he liked it. If he screwed up, he didn't have to answer to anyone but himself.

Howard Lee drove into the hospital parking lot and parked in his usual space. He reached across the seat and got his lunch bucket from the passenger seat, then grabbed his cap as he got out of the van, taking care to lock it before heading for the employee entrance of Savannah Memorial. The shift change was already in progress as he reached his locker.

"Hey, Martin…how's it going?"

Howard Lee nodded and waved as he got his coveralls off the shelf. He wanted to share the news of his new family with the man, but couldn't take the chance. Not here. Not now. Maybe when they moved it would be better. And he'd been thinking about the move all evening. Even though his Sophie was still in a stage of revolt, it would pass, just like it did with his girls. Of course Amy Anne had gone a little too far the other way, but she would come back when she was ready.

He put on his coveralls, then began to fill his cart with cleaning supplies, making sure he had everything he would need to work his shift before heading for the employee elevator. A couple of women waved at him—one even stopped and spoke a few words. Her name was Mavis. He liked to be part of the machine that ran the hospital even though his education was barely enough to qualify him for cleaning toilets.

The elevator finally arrived and he pushed his cart forward. Mavis followed with her own cart as she continued to talk.

"Did you hear about the break-in on Pediatrics?"

Howard Lee's heartbeat broke rhythm, but only for a moment. There was no way they would know it was him.

"No, I didn't. When did it happen?"

"Earlier this morning, a little before nine."

"Oh...well, I clocked out at seven. I guess that's why I hadn't heard."

"Yeah, me too, but my sister is a nurse on four. She called and told me! Can you believe it?"

Howard Lee shook his head. He didn't really want to get into a conversation about the crime, especially since he was the one who'd committed it.

"Well, here's my floor."

"See you later," she said, and smiled a goodbye as Howard Lee pushed his cart off the elevator onto the Pediatric ward, then headed for the first room on the right.

It was a simple job—one he could perform without thought, leaving his mind free to entertain scenarios of him and his new family—picturing the evening meals together around the table. And the holidays. He couldn't wait for the holidays. Maybe he'd dress up like Santa Claus. The girls would love it, he was sure.

He reached room 301 and pushed the cart up against the wall, grabbed a handful of trash bags as he entered.

The door was open. The two-bed room had only one occupant—a young boy with no hair. Howard Lee knew he was a cancer patient. He also knew the boy was dying. He headed for the bathrooms without looking at the boy, nodding only briefly to the sad-eyed parent sitting quietly at the bedside. He changed out the trash cans, refilled the paper towel holders and made sure there was sufficient antibacterial soap in the dispenser. Then he went to his cart, got the big dust mop from the rack and ran it over the cold, white-tiled floor, making sure to keep his head down and his thoughts to himself. The moment he was through, he was on to the next, taking comfort in the mindless routine of the job.

It wasn't until he neared the nurses' station that his equilibrium shifted. They were talking about the theft. He smiled as he worked, silently congratulating himself on his prowess when one of the nurses saw him and called out.

"Mr. Martin...we're out of paper cups in the break room. Could you bring up a carton?"

"Yes, certainly," he said.

The nurse smiled her thanks and went back to her paperwork. Moments later, the desk phone rang. Howard Lee was still nearby when he heard her answer.

"Pediatrics. Nurse Hanson. Yes sir...send him up, we'll be waiting."

She hung up, then called to a nurse who was coming out of a nearby room.

"Security's coming up to pull the tapes," she said. "I've got to go down to 356. Will you wait and escort them into the drug room?"

"Sure," the nurse said, and moved behind the desk.

Howard Lee straightened abruptly and turned toward the nurses' station then to the room beyond. Tapes? What tapes?

He searched the hallways with a frantic gaze, looking for signs of security cameras, but saw nothing that would put him on alert. He'd been so sure of the territory in which he worked he hadn't thought past the need to get medicine for the girls. But in doing so, he'd moved beyond his safety zone into a place he'd never been, and so might have signed his own arrest warrant.

He grabbed his cart, all but running as he started pushing it toward the employee elevator. Sweat was running down his back and his stomach was rolling in panic as he waited impatiently for the car to arrive. Behind him, he heard the ding as the public elevator stopped on third, heard the near-silent swish as the doors slid inward. He wouldn't turn. He couldn't look. He just held his breath and prayed.

Moments later the employee elevator arrived. The moment the doors opened, he was shoving the cart inside. He fought nausea all the way down to the basement, and the moment the car stopped he was out and running. He shoved his cart into an alcove, stripped off his coveralls and bolted for the exit.

"Hey, Martin...where are you going?" someone yelled.

Howard Lee never answered and didn't look back. He was all the way to the van before he realized he'd left his lunch box in the fridge. He hesitated, wondering if he should go back and retrieve it and then decided against it. There was nothing in it to incriminate him, although he wondered why he cared. He'd already taken care of that by stealing drugs in full view of his employer's security cameras.

His hands were shaking as he unlocked the van and jumped inside.

"Oh God...oh God...oh God."

He jammed the key in the ignition and started the engine, then paused for a moment with his head on the steering wheel. What was he going to do? Yes, he'd planned on moving, but not now. Not without proper planning.

There was a sudden and sharp rap on the window. He jerked. A security guard was standing beside his van. *God!*

"Hey, buddy...are you okay?"

Certain he was about to be arrested, Howard Lee gunned the engine and peeled out of the parking lot, barely missing the toes of the stunned security guard. He needed to get home. All he had to do was get home, then he would be safe. Safe with his girls...and his bride.

Chapter 12

Mary tiptoed out of the bathroom, her skin still damp from the shower. She didn't know what time it was because her watch had been broken when she'd been tossed into the van, but she kept feeling an overwhelming need to wash. It had something to do with being abducted—the mental trauma that rape victims go through in a constant need to wash their abductor's touch from their bodies.

At the thought of rape, she shuddered. She couldn't let herself go there. Whatever else she might still endure was up to God, Daniel and the police. All she could hope was that whatever Howard Lee did to her, he didn't do it in front of the girls.

She tugged at her rumpled clothes, wishing for something clean to put on, then noticed the two little girls had finally gone to sleep. Since her arrival, she'd put them both in one bed, leaving the other bed for herself. Although she was sick at heart about being abducted, and could only imagine the hell that Daniel and Hope must be going through, she didn't regret being here. Now that she'd seen Justine and Amy Anne, she couldn't bear to think of them alone with this man or what he'd made them endure.

She moved to their bedside. Amy Anne might not have much to say when she was awake, but there was obviously a part of her that was still fighting. Her covers were a mess—wadded at the foot of the bed and in a tangle beneath her feet. Justine slept with her face toward the wall with Amy Anne curled up behind her. Mary couldn't help but think that putting the girls in bed together had been inspired. Before, Amy Anne had refused to instigate any form of communication. Now, she slept with her arm slung around Justine and her nose buried in the middle of her back.

Mary could only imagine the fear their parents must be going through and wished they knew the girls were alive and no longer alone. Exhaustion hit as she bent down to untangle the covers. Her hands were trembling as she straightened the sheets and pulled them back over the girls. It made her think of her nightly ritual with Hope. Instead of going straight to bed, she turned back to the girls.

"Good night, sweet babies," she said softly, kissed them each on the cheek.

She would like nothing better than to strip down to bare skin and crawl between the sheets, but there was no way she would risk being found naked by Howard Lee. He had decided she was going to be the girls' mother. The last thing she needed was for him to decide she would also be his wife.

She started to lay down, then glanced toward the

stairwell and frowned. She was so exhausted, but was afraid to close her eyes. What if he came down here while she was sleeping and took one of the girls?

She looked back toward the beds, studying the lay-out of the room, and then grabbed the foot of her bed and pulled, angling it until it was abutted firmly against the other bed with no space between. Now if Howard Lee tried to get to the girls, he would have to go over her to do it.

Her shoulders slumped as she sat down and kicked off her shoes. Last night she'd slept in Daniel's arms. Who could have known that tonight she would sleep in hell?

Finally, she stretched out. Wincing from sore mus-cles, she pulled the covers up over her legs and then scooted backward until she could feel the warmth of the girls' bodies against her back.

The shadows from the nightlights cast strange shapes against the walls. She watched, half-expecting them to come to life and decimate what was left of her sanity, but they remained in place. Finally she was satisfied that, for the moment, they were alone and safe. At that point, she began to relax. Just before she drifted off to sleep, something occurred to her that she'd never thought of before.

Maybe there had been more than one reason why she'd been sent back in time. Maybe it wasn't all about being given a second chance with Daniel and Hope. She distinctly remembered that day—the day everything had changed. She'd been standing at the stop light, half-listening to the conversation that the two women had been having about the three missing children. Right after that, she'd found the antique shop and gone inside.

Mary had finally accepted the unbelievable fact that she'd gone back in time and changed the outcome of her own fate, as well as Daniel and Hope's. But in coming back, she'd also changed the fate of these children, as well. Unless Howard Lee had a third child stashed in another location, she'd changed his future, too, because he'd taken her, and not another little girl. And because Hope hadn't died when she was a child, she'd lived to give the police a description of the man responsible for the abductions.

Once, Mary might have thought these notions farfetched, but not now. Satisfied that she was in the right place whether she liked it or not, she snuggled a little farther beneath her covers and closed her eyes, unaware that their fragile world was about to shatter.

It had started to rain—a soft, gentle shower that fell on the pavement and turned the puddles into psychedelic mirrors for the illumination from the streetlights above. Howard Lee drove with a patent disregard for rules, running through yellow lights, taking corners on two wheels, and sending up the occasional spray of water from beneath the van's tires. His thoughts were scattered, his equilibrium shot. Had his mother still been alive, she would have predicted that he'd react in such a manner. Howard Lee had never taken surprises well.

When he was about ten blocks from home, he saw the lights of an all-night ATM. Impulsively, he exited the street and turned toward the drive-thru, coming to a halt in front of the machine. Twice, he tried to get his wallet out of his pocket and both times it slipped out of his grasp. He took a deep breath, wiped the sweat from the palms of his hands onto his pants legs, and then reached for the wallet again. Finally, he got the ATM card and thrust it into the slot, entered his PIN number and took five hundred dollars out of his account. Once he had the cash in hand, he tried to repeat the process but was denied. Cursing the safeguard his bank had put on his own account, he pocketed the money and drove back onto the streets, heading for home.

Minutes later, he pulled into his driveway, hit the garage door opener, and drove inside. Only after the door was down and the engine off, did he take a deep breath. His heart was still hammering, but he was beginning to regain focus.

He was home. The familiarity of his surroundings calmed his panic. He took another deep breath and got out of the van. The sounds of his footsteps echoed loudly within the roomy old garage and he caught himself tiptoeing into the house, then cursed his foolishness. There was nothing to be afraid of here. This was his territory. Here was where he made the rules.

He moved into the kitchen, quickly locking the door behind him, and then headed for the living room, gave the front door a quick tug to make sure it was locked, too, then paused.

This wasn't the way he'd planned their future, but plans were made to be changed. He patted his pocket, taking some assurance from the fat wad of bills he'd just withdrawn from the bank, and headed for the bedroom. As he started down the hall, he paused at the door to the guest bedroom, remembering all the preparations he'd made for the arrival of his new daughter, and frowned. After a moment, he sighed, reminding himself that the plan had already changed and the world hadn't come to an end. In fact, things were already better now that his girls had a mother to look after them when he was at work.

Then his frown deepened. Besides getting out of town, he was going to have to find a new job and possibly a new identity. This was a setback he hadn't planned on, but he would find a way to make it work. He had to.

He shrugged off his jacket and dropped it on the back of a chair as he moved across the hall into his bedroom. There were things to be done and not a lot of time to do them. He kicked away the throw rug over the cellar door and then took a key out of his pocket and unlocked the padlock. Halfway down the stairs, he knew something was different. By the time he reached the bottom, he was frowning.

Mary was on her feet, standing between him and the bed where the girls were sleeping.

"Sophie…why aren't you asleep?"

"Stop calling me that," she said sharply. "As for not being asleep, I'm guessing you're curious as to why I'm not doped out of my mind, right?"

His frown deepened. How could she know this so quickly? What kind of a woman had he brought into his home?

"What are you?" he asked.

Mary took a step forward. "The biggest mistake you ever made."

For the second time tonight his fear spiked.

"Don't threaten me," he said, and pointed a finger toward her. "I'm the one in charge." Then he glanced toward the girls, who were obviously no longer asleep, either. "So you choose to sleep on your terms? Fine. But you will live on mine, so I suggest you put our girls back to bed and get some rest. Tomorrow is going to be a very busy day.''

"Why? What's so special about tomorrow?" Mary asked.

Howard Lee smiled. "Why…we're moving, that's what. I think it's time for a change of scenery, don't you? After all, you said it yourself. The girls need a more comfortable and healthy environment. I intend to see that they get what they need.''

He pivoted quickly and took the stairs up two at a time. The cellar door was down and locked before Mary could react. She felt as helpless now as she had when he'd thrown her in the van. Filled with despair, she dropped down on the bed and covered her face with her hands.

No…oh no…if he takes us away, Daniel might never find us. Please Lord…help me stop him before it's too late.

"Don't cry, Mary.''

Mary looked up just as Justine crawled into her lap. She wrapped her arms around the little girl. Once again, she was struck by how strong the spirit could be in such a tiny child.

"I'm not crying, honey. I'm just tired. How about you?''

Justine nodded, then pointed to Amy Anne. "She's sleepy, too, aren't you, Amy Anne?''

Mary turned around. Amy Anne was sitting cross-legged in the bed, picking at a raveling thread on the blanket. She held her breath, hoping that Amy Anne would talk. She didn't get the words, but she did get a brief moment of eye contact before Amy Anne nodded.

"Okay..." she said. "Then let's get some sleep, what do you say?"

"Is the man going to come back?" Justine asked.

"I don't think so. At least not again tonight. But you don't worry. I'm here and I won't let anything happen to you again."

She gave each little girl a hug and then started tucking them back beneath the covers before stretching out in front of them, using her body as a shield between them and Howard Lee.

She was almost asleep when she felt the brush of a small hand against her arm. Tears welled behind her eyelids as she felt the hesitancy of the touch. Justine was too far away to reach her like this. It had to be Amy Anne. Without speaking, she reached for the tiny fingers and then covered them with her own. There was a moment when she thought she felt hesitance, then quietly, without disturbing the covers, Mary felt the child scooting just a tiny bit closer.

For now, it was enough.

It was raining. Daniel stood at the living room window, watching it fall and praying with every breath in his body that Mary was still alive. There was a growing ache in his gut and what felt like a permanent knot at the back of his throat. He kept alternating with the need to break something or break down and cry. Bobby Joe had gone home hours earlier with a promise to pick him up first thing in the morning, and now he was left alone with the horror of his reality.

He glanced at his watch. It was ten minutes after two in the morning. He needed to sleep, but resting while Mary was missing seemed somehow disloyal.

However, tomorrow would be hell if he didn't. Reluctantly, he went upstairs to their room and laid down on the bed without undressing. Within minutes, he'd succumbed to exhaustion.

"Daniel...come and get me."

"Mary? Mary? Is that you?"

Daniel turned toward the sound of her voice, trying desperately to fight his way out of the dream.

"We're alive, Daniel. We're all alive."

"Who's we?"

"Me and Justine and Amy Anne, but we're running out of time. Please, Danny...come and get us before Howard Lee takes us away. We want to go home."

Daniel woke with a gasp and sat straight up in bed.

"Mary?"

He'd said her name out of reflex, although he hadn't expected an answer. He knew he'd been dreaming, but it wasn't like any dream he'd ever had. It seemed as if he'd heard her as clearly as if she'd been lying right beside him. As for the mention of the two little girls, that was weird. What had she called them? Oh yeah...Justine and Amy Anne. And Howard Lee? Who the hell was Howard Lee?

Dismissing it as nothing more than part of the nightmare in which they were caught, he still made a mental note of the names. He would call Reese Arnaud tomorrow and see if any progress had been made. Chances are he'd heard the girls' names on the news and then forgotten them until his subconscious had drawn them up into his dream. As for a man named Howard Lee, he couldn't believe it meant anything. As much as he wanted to think he and Mary were soul mates, he didn't believe in psychic communication.

Too awake now to go back to sleep, he got out of bed and walked to the window. It was still raining. The wet streets had taken on a look of obsidian—their dark, mirrored surfaces a reflection of his soul.

Time passed slowly, and still he couldn't get the sound of Mary's voice out of his mind. It had been so vivid, and the dream so specific. If only he dared believe. He swiped a hand over his face and then turned away from the windows, and as he did, his gaze fell on the bed. It was so damned big—and too empty without her.

Without warning, he started to cry. *Please God, don't let me spend the rest of my life without her in it.*

Reese Arnaud was at his desk by 5:00 a.m., pouring over the computer printout that had come from the Department of Motor Vehicles. He couldn't believe how many people in the city of Savannah owned white vans. He'd quit counting at four hundred and thirty-seven. What was frightening was the thought that the man they were looking for might not even be a resident of Georgia. If that was the case, then the names on this list could be moot.

He poured himself a third cup of coffee as he downed the last bite of his sausage biscuit, then flopped back in his chair. Someone told him yesterday that Bobby Joe Killian was asking questions at the supermarket where Mary O'Rourke had been abducted and that Daniel was with him. It didn't make his job any easier to know that the man he called his friend didn't trust him to bring his wife home. That he had turned to a P.I. with a less than perfect reputation made it worse. Then he frowned. That wasn't entirely the truth. Truth was, Reese couldn't blame him. The little girls had been missing for more than six weeks, and they hadn't had a solid lead until the sketch. If it was his wife, he wouldn't want to wait in the wings, either. He'd be turning over every known perp on the streets and yanking until one of them squealed.

Heartsick and exhausted, he took a long drink of the coffee and then went back to the list, marking off all the names of owners with vans that were more than ten years old.

A short while later, his phone rang. He picked it up without thought, his focus still on the pages.

"Savannah P.D."

"Arnaud…this is Williams in Vice. Got a little piece of video with a person on it you might want to see."

"Unless she's six feet tall and naked, I don't think so," Reese muttered.

The detective chuckled, then dropped another line that got Reese's attention.

"It's not a she, it's a he, and he's stealing medicine from the third floor of Savannah Memorial."

"What's that got to do with me?" Reese asked.

"Well, one of the guys here in Vice thought the perp looked a little like that man in the sketch you've been circulating."

Reese stood abruptly. "I'm on my way."

A short while later Reese was sitting alongside Detective Williams, as well as two other detectives, viewing the tape.

"What do you think?" Williamson asked.

Reese leaned forward, resting his elbows on his knees. Holding the remote, he hit Rewind, then Play. It was the fourth time he'd viewed the piece of tape and still he couldn't be sure.

"I don't know," Reese said. "The tape quality is poor. The images are grainy. It's a tall, blond man, but we don't have a real clear view of his face."

"Yeah, I know," Williams said. "But you don't see a crazy haircut like that every day."

Reese nodded, eyeing the man's bone-straight hair. Williams was right about that. It looked like someone had turned a bowl upside down on his head and trimmed off everything that stuck out from under it.

"I'd feel better about it if he'd smiled for the camera," Reese muttered.

Williams frowned. "What?"

"Oh, nothing," Reese said. "It's just that he's supposed to have this goofy set of teeth. Distinctive enough to set him aside from the crowd, you know?"

"Yeah, okay. So what do you want to do about this?" Williams asked.

Reese frowned. "What does the hospital have to say about the tape? Anyone there identified the man?"

"They've shown it to the nurses on the third floor, but identification is a bust. Supposedly he looks like someone named Barry, who's an ex-husband of one RN. Also, someone else said he looks like their brother, but that's a dead-end too because the brother is in the Navy and stationed in the Black Sea. Another said he looked a little like one of the janitors, but that man wasn't even on duty when the robbery went down."

Reese thought of the janitor angle. It made sense.

"It has to be someone who knew the layout of the floor," Reese said.

"Why do you say that?"

"Because my daughter, Molly, had her tonsils out there two years ago. They only have minimal medications on site. The main pharmacy for the hospital is on the first floor."

Williams glared at the two detectives nearby. "Why does he know that and we don't?"

They shrugged and grinned.

"What did he steal?" Reese asked.

Williams looked at his notes. "Some antibiotics. No hard drugs like you would expect."

"What kind of antibiotics?" Reese asked.

"Ummm...ampicillin and something I can't pronounce that the doctor said is used for people who are allergic to penicillin. Also, some hypodermic syringes."

"Oh damn," Reese said, and got up from the chair.

"What?" Williams asked.

"One of the little girls who's missing...she's allergic to penicillin. Her mother says she was wearing a Medic Alert bracelet."

"Oh man...if this is the guy who took them and he's stealing medicine, then that means the girls are sick."

Reese grinned. "No...it means that the girls are alive."

"Oh yeah...right!" Williams said. "So what are you going to do?"

"Before we jump to too many conclusions, I need a list of employees at the hospital and I want the clerk at the supermarket to look at this tape. If she thinks it's the man who snatched Mary O'Rourke, then at least we'll know we're looking for the same perp for all three abductions.''

Bobby Joe Killian swerved off the street and into the drive in front of Daniel's house. He stomped the brakes, leaving a streak of black rubber on the pavement as he killed the engine.

Daniel was coming out of the house before Bobby Joe could get out of the car.

"Hurry," Bobby Joe said.

"Why?" Daniel asked, as he slid into the seat.

"You know that pretty little clerk at the supermarket?"

"The one who witnessed Mary's abduction?"

"Yep."

"What about her?" Daniel asked.

"She's going on her way to the police station to look at a tape."

"A tape of what?"

"Not sure," Bobby Joe said, as he peeled out of the driveway and back onto the street.

"How do you know this?" Daniel asked.

Bobby Joe grinned. "We were still in her bed when she got the call."

"You slept with her?"

Bobby Joe shrugged. "Yeah, why not? She's pretty, she's single and she asked."

"Isn't that some kind of conflict of interest?" Daniel asked.

"Not for me," Bobby Joe said.

"Yeah, right. What was I thinking?"

Chapter 13

Reese was still in Detective Williams's office, waiting for the supermarket clerk to arrive when Bobby Joe and Daniel showed up. His first instinct was to give Daniel a hard time for getting mixed up with Killian, and then he looked at his face. The man looked haunted. It was enough to temper his greeting.

"You guys lost?" he asked.

"I want to see the security tape from the hospital robbery," Daniel said.

Reese didn't bother to hide his surprise. "How the hell did you find out about that?"

"A little birdie named Carol told me," Bobby Joe said.

Detective Williams eyebrows shot up toward his hairline. "You know Carol Shane?"

"Intimately."

"Well hell, Killian, is there no woman safe from you in the city of Savannah?"

Bobby Joe grinned. "I have yet to hear a complaint."

Ignoring the byplay between Williams and Killian, Reese turned to Daniel.

"Look, friend, I understand where you're coming from, but trust me, it won't make you feel a damn bit better to see it. We're not even sure the man we've got on film is the same one who took Mary."

Before Daniel could answer, another detective yelled from across the room.

"Hey, Williams. There's a woman here named Carol Shane who says you're expecting her."

They all turned to look at the young blonde who was waiting in the doorway. Williams got up to go meet her, but Bobby Joe beat him to it. In seconds, he was at the door and kissing the woman on the cheek.

Williams snorted beneath his breath. "He's a real piece of work, isn't he?"

"He's a friend," Daniel said. "He came when I called."

Williams looked taken aback. "I didn't mean anything by it. It's just—"

"Never mind," Daniel said. "It doesn't matter. Nothing matters but getting Mary back."

"And those two little girls," Reese added.

"If they're still alive," a detective remarked.

Daniel shoved his hands in his pockets and then looked at the floor. When he spoke it was so low, Reese had to lean forward to hear him.

"According to Mary, they're still alive," Daniel muttered.

Reese jerked as if he'd been hit.

"What the hell do you mean? Have you talked to her? Did you get a ransom call?"

"No, no, nothing like that," Daniel said. "I shouldn't have said anything. Forget it."

"Damn it, Daniel, talk to me."

"Look, I dreamed it, okay?"

"What do you mean, you dreamed it?"

"Last night...I saw Mary. She was telling me she was okay and that the girls were alive. She said Justine and Amy Anne. Are those their names?"

Reese paled. "Yeah. But you could have heard that on the news and forgotten it until last night in your sleep."

Daniel nodded. "I know. It was just so real."

Williams yelled at Bobby Joe. "Hey, Killian. Save the Romeo stuff for later and escort Ms. Shane to the front row-seat we've saved for her."

Bobby Joe cupped a hand underneath the woman's elbow and walked her across the room. "Detectives...this is Carol Shane. Be nice. She's nervous, okay?"

Williams glared at Bobby Joe and then helped the woman to a chair in front of the TV and VCR.

"Ms. Shane, we appreciate you coming in like this. There's no reason to be afraid, and the tape we want you to see is very brief. There's nothing violent on it. Just a man going in and then leaving a room. What I want you to do is look at his face and tell us if he's the same man who abducted Mary O'Rourke yesterday."

She glanced nervously at each of the men and then nodded before fixing her gaze on the blank television screen. Williams hit the remote and immediately, the screen was filled with images from the robbery.

Daniel tensed as Carol Shane leaned forward, and like before, they replayed the same bit of footage several times before they asked for her answer.

"Well, Ms. Shane, what do you think?" Reese asked.

Carol looked up. "I can't be sure, but it certainly looked like him. Not many people wear their hair like that, and although there wasn't a real good shot of his face, I'd say it was him."

"Are you sure?" Williams asked. "Remember, you only got a brief look at him yesterday at the supermarket."

Bobby Joe stepped forward and laid a hand on Carol's back.

"Oh no, that's not exactly true, is it, honey?"

"What do you mean?" Reese asked.

Carol was fidgeting with the hem of her T-shirt as she looked up at the men ringed around her.

"Well, it's like I told Bobby Joe last night...the man who took that woman...uh...he's a regular in the store."

Reese cursed beneath his breath. "Why don't we know this?"

Carol Shane looked like she was going to cry.

"I told the first officer on the scene that I'd seen him before, but that I didn't know his name."

"Tell him what else you told me, honey," Bobby Joe urged. "You know...about what he's been buying."

"Oh! That!" Carol said. "I've been working at Vinter's for almost a year and I've seen him off and on from the start. Only he used to buy stuff like a single man buys. You know...frozen dinners, Hamburger Helper, stuff like that. Only lately he's started buying stuff like people buy when they have kids.''

"Like what?" Reese asked.

"Like fun cereal with marshmallows in it and different juices and lots of milk. Oh…and frozen chicken nuggets, weiners, little individual kid snacks.''

"Did he ever say anything to you?"

Carol shook her head. "No. He doesn't even look at me. Just looks down, digs the money out of his wallet and leaves.''

"Can you remember him ever paying by check?"

"Not to me.''

"How can you be sure?" Daniel asked.

"Because I know a lot of my regulars and he's the only one I used to see fairly often that I didn't know by name.''

Reese stood, and then helped Carol Shane to her feet.

"Okay, Ms. Shane. Thank you so much for coming in. If you remember anything else, please give me a call.'' He handed her his card and then nodded at Bobby Joe.

Bobby Joe winked at Daniel. "Be right back," he said, and walked her out of the office.

Daniel turned to Reese. "So what do you think?"

"I think we're probably looking at the same man.''

"And…''

Reese frowned. "Without a name, we're right back where we were this morning. We're looking for a man who drives a white van. The fact that he's buying kid food at a supermarket and stealing antibiotics that one would ordinarily administer to children only tells me that the girls are probably alive. The fact that he's stealing medicine isn't a good sign that the girls are well, but at least they're still breathing. That's more than we knew two days ago.''

Daniel shoved a hand through his hair in frustration.

''How many names on the DMV list?''

''You don't want to know,'' Reese muttered.

''Actually, yes I do,'' Daniel said. ''I'm dying here.''

Reese put a hand on his friend's shoulder, wishing there was something he could say that would help, but there was not.

Then Daniel looked up, unashamed of the tears blurring his vision.

''Find her, Reese. Please.''

''I'm doing my best, Daniel.''

Daniel's mouth twisted into something between a grimace and a smile.

''Last night…in my dream…''

''Yeah, what about it?'' Reese asked.

''Mary called the man Howard Lee.''

Reese's eyes widened. ''Hell. You dreamed that, too?''

Daniel shrugged. ''I didn't dream it. It's what she said. Howard Lee.''

''Yeah, right,'' Reese said, then he added. ''There's one other thing Carol Shane said that should help us eliminate some more names on the DMV list.''

''What's that?'' Daniel asked.

''If he shops in that supermarket regularly, then he must live in the general area. We'll keep that in mind when we're going through the list.''

Bobby Joe Killian walked into the room. Daniel knew about his bad-boy image, but he didn't care. He was also relentless.

"Let us help," Daniel begged.

Reese frowned. "No. Absolutely not. This is a police matter."

"Fine," Daniel said. "Just know that we're going to be looking anyway, whether you like it or not."

"Damn it, Daniel, you're making my job harder."

"Then don't shut me out," Daniel said. "Bobby Joe is a licensed private investigator. He's already got the same list from the DMV that you have. We can either work together and maybe find Mary and those girls before it's too late, or you can keep stalling me and make everything take twice as long."

"He's right, you know," Bobby Joe said.

Reese turned. "You're back already? Surely you weren't gone long enough to get her phone number and address?"

"Already been there, done that," he said. "So are you going to let us help or do we go maverick on you?"

"I should lock you both up," Reese said.

"No, let's find the bastard and lock him up, instead," Bobby Joe said.

Reese threw his hands up in disgust.

"Okay, fine," Reese said. "We'll divide up the list. If you find someone suspicious, you call it in. You don't play cowboy and go after him on your own."

Daniel shook his head. "No deal. If we find him, we'll call it in, but if he has Mary, he's mine."

Howard Lee's phone began to ring just as he was putting bacon in the frying pan. He looked at the caller ID as he wiped his hands and then frowned. Savannah Memorial. Someone from work was calling him. This wasn't good. Not once in his entire time with the hospital had anyone ever called before.

He let the phone ring as he went back to breakfast. Time was precious. If he did what instinct told him to do, he'd already be gone. But the girls had been sick and he'd been afraid to yank them out of their beds without rest and food.

He turned the fire down under the skillet and then took some eggs from the fridge and began breaking them into a bowl. Normally, he would have served the girls cereal, but there was no telling how long it would be before he could take a chance and stop to feed them. They needed a good, solid meal before the journey began.

As he popped bread into the toaster, he thought of Sophie and frowned. If she'd been a good wife, she would be the one making breakfast. But he couldn't trust her. Instead, he had to keep her shut up with the girls.

He turned the bacon and then took glasses from the cabinet and filled them with milk. He started to put sedatives in the milk so that the girls would be complacent on the trip, and then realized that Sophie probably wouldn't let them drink it. She'd obviously tossed their drinks the night before. He discarded the thought, reminding himself that he could easily give it to them later in a soft drink before they left.

As for Sophie, he didn't know exactly what he was going to do with her, but he damned sure wasn't taking her along.

A short while later he started down the stairs with

their food on a tray, taking care not to spill as he maneuvered the narrow opening. As he got to the bottom step, he saw the beds were empty. He started to frown and then noticed the bathroom door was shut.

"Breakfast," he called out.

The bathroom door opened almost instantly and Mary looked out.

"We'll be there in a minute."

He set the food down on the table and then started toward the bathroom.

"Is there a problem?" he asked.

"No. The girls are getting out of the tub. They're just not dressed yet."

"I can help," he said, and started to push the door wider when Mary put a hand in the middle of his chest and pushed him backward.

"You don't touch these girls again," she said. "God only knows what you've already done to them."

Howard Lee paled. The idea that he would be improper with his daughters was appalling.

"I've done nothing wrong!" he cried, and then yanked Mary out of the doorway, shaking her roughly as he shouted in her face. "You're evil for even thinking such a thing."

Mary flinched. His features had twisted into an angry grimace and the grip he had on her arms was beginning to hurt, but couldn't let him see her fear. She tore out of his grasp and then put herself between him and bathroom, where the girls were still dressing.

"You're the one who's evil," she snapped. "How can you stand there and tell me you've done nothing wrong? You stole these children! You locked them up in this...this...dungeon, and then you drugged them senseless. My God! Have you no shame? Have you no conscience? Don't you care that they weep for their parents? They're not your daughters, they're your captives...just like I am."

Howard Lee was livid. He didn't want to hear this. He wouldn't listen to the lies anymore.

"You're wrong!" he shouted. "They're mine. But you can quit worrying about yourself. I don't want you around them anymore. We're leaving...but you're not. Do you hear me, woman?" Then he pointed to the table. "Get the children out here and make sure they eat a proper meal. And please see that they drink their milk. I did not put any medicine in it, although when I come back, I will have to administer another shot of antibiotic to each of them."

"I don't want no shot."

They both turned. Justine was standing in the doorway, holding Amy Anne's hand. "Neither does Amy Anne."

Howard Lee's mood darkened even more. He did not like dissension.

"Shut up! All of you!" he yelled. "I've got things to do and clothes to pack. Sit down and eat your food. I'll be back in a while to help you pack your things. Then we're going on a trip."

"I don't want to go on a trip, either," Justine said. "I want to stay with Mary."

Mary moved to the children and then pulled them close. It angered Howard Lee to see how they clung to her.

"Do as I say!" he ordered, and then stalked back

up the stairs, slamming the door shut with a ferocious thud.

"He's good and mad," Justine said.

Mary shuddered. "Yes, he is," she said, and then made herself smile. "Come on girls, lets eat some breakfast. We've got to keep our strength up. And while we eat, we need to make a plan. Okay?"

They nodded and then followed her to the table. It did Mary good to see both girls tuck into the food. While she wasn't so sure about their future, hers looked even worse. If he didn't plan to take her with him, then what? Would he just leave her locked up in here, or would he kill her?

She took a bite of the toast and then helped the girls spread jelly on theirs. Justine dug into the food with the exuberance of youth, confident that with Mary as their ally, she would make everything all right. Amy Anne was more hesitant, but with Mary's help, ate her food, too. Mary was glad that they believed in her. It would make things easier, but she wished she had as much confidence in herself. Dear God, she wanted to go home.

Daniel stood against the car with his arms crossed, waiting for Bobby Joe to finish talking to the woman across the street. She was the eighth person on the list that they'd talked to since they'd left the precinct and so far, no luck. He took his cell phone out of his pocket and called his parents. He needed to hear Hope's voice and to reassure her that everything was all right. So far, she had no idea her mother was missing and he wanted to keep it that way. A few seconds later, his mother answered.

"Mom, it's me. How's Hope?"

"She's fine. She's having a ball and knows nothing about what's going on."

Daniel looked down at the toe of his boot, concentrating on the scuff marks to keep from losing his mind.

"Good. Is she with Dad?"

"Yes, they went to the park."

Unconsciously, his shoulders slumped. He'd wanted to talk to her, but it was probably better that he didn't. It was getting harder and harder to hide his emotions.

"Okay...good."

"Do you have any news?" Phyllis asked.

"Well, we know that the same guy who snatched Mary is probably the man who took the two little girls who are missing."

"My God!" Phyllis gasped. "Are they...do you know if—"

"We're pretty sure they're alive because he was caught on tape stealing some antibiotics from the hospital. The doctors said it was stuff normally given to children. One of the medicines he stole is a substitute for people who are allergic to penicillin and one of the little girls who is missing is allergic to it. A lot of this is circumstantial guesswork, but it's pretty close to the mark."

"I'm so sorry," Phyllis said.

"So am I, Mom. So am I." Then his voice shook. "I can't do this without her."

"Do what?" Phyllis asked.

"Live." He choked back a sob. "I can't even imagine my life without her."

"Then don't," Phyllis said shortly. "Think positive, darling."

"Yeah...well...tell Hope I called, okay? And I don't know how long this is going to take so—"

"Don't worry about it. If you haven't found her by Monday, we'll see that Hope gets to school."

"Monday is October the 2nd...Hope's birthday."

"Oh, we know. She's already reminded us a dozen times. Had Mary planned a party?"

Daniel frowned, remembering how pale Mary had gotten in the antique shop before she'd passed out, and how confused she'd been for a while afterward.

"No, not really. She hadn't been feeling too well the past few days."

"Don't worry," she said. "We'll make a big deal out of the day for her, although you know if Mary is still gone then, you're going to have to tell her something. She'll expect her mother to be present on her birthday."

Hell. "What if she's not?"

"One thing at a time, dear. For now, she's fine. Who knows? Maybe you'll get a break in the case."

"From your lips to God's ears," Daniel muttered.

"Goodbye, honey. If you need anything, just let us know."

"Yeah, all right, Mom. And thanks."

"No thanks are necessary."

He disconnected and dropped the cell phone back in his pocket as Bobby Joe came running to the car.

"Any luck?" Daniel asked.

"Nope. Who's next on the list?"

"I don't know. I'll look as you drive."

They got inside the car. Bobby Joe started the engine as Daniel took the list from the dashboard. He marked off the name from the address they'd just left and then ran his finger down the paper to the next one.

"Uh...a Delmar Watts on—"

But Daniel didn't finish what he'd been going to say.

"What's wrong?" Bobby Joe asked.

"This," Daniel said, pointing to a name farther down on the page.

"What about it?"

"Howard Lee Martin. It says Howard Lee Martin, 1449 Raleigh Avenue."

"So? Do you know him?"

Daniel shivered suddenly, as if a ghost had just walked past his ear.

"No."

"Then what's the big deal?"

Daniel looked up, his face devoid of all expression.

"Last night in my dream, Mary called the man Howard Lee."

Bobby Joe pulled to the curb and then turned and looked at Daniel.

"Well hell," he said softly.

"Exactly."

Bobby Joe frowned. "Do you believe in precognition?"

Daniel shook his head. "No, but I believe in Mary Faith."

"That's good enough for me," Bobby Joe said. "What street did you say he lived on?"

"Raleigh. 1449 Raleigh."

"Hand me the city map."

Daniel did as he was asked, watching anxiously as

Bobby Joe scanned the map. The longer he sat, the more certain he felt that this meant something.

"Hurry," he said.

Bobby Joe looked up.

"Is there something you're not telling me?" he asked.

"Just hurry."

Bobby Joe slammed the car in gear and peeled away from the curb, leaving a short streak of black rubber on the pavement behind him.

Daniel braced himself and hung on.

Reese Arnaud pulled the last sheet from the fax machine and dropped it on the desk next to the list from the DMV. It was a complete listing of every employee from Savannah Memorial. Now he had to see if any of the names cross-matched with the names from the DMV. He sat down with a thump, shifted the lists so that they were side by side, then started reading.

He was halfway through the list from Savannah General when one of the names jumped out at him. He frowned, trying to remember why the name Howard Lee Martin would mean anything, and then it hit him. Daniel's dream! He said Mary had told him the man name's was Howard Lee.

He shivered suddenly, and then dug through the DMV list, telling himself the name wouldn't—no, couldn't—be there, too. But it was. Howard Lee Martin. 1449 Raleigh Avenue.

Reese reached for a city map, looking to see where Raleigh Street was in conjunction with Vinter's supermarket.

"Son of a bitch," he said softly, and then stood.

"Patrick...come with me," he yelled.

"Where are we going?" the detective asked, as he got up from his desk.

"I'm not sure," Reese muttered. "But I'm desperate enough to give this a try."

Chapter 14

All during breakfast, Mary was encouraged by Amy Anne's behavior. Twice during the meal she'd caught the little girl watching her when she thought she wasn't looking. While she was encouraged by Amy Anne's improvement, Mary wasn't sure if she was strong enough to go through with her plan.

After Howard Lee's threat, Mary had been given no choice. She had to make a move before Howard Lee separated her from the girls. If he got away from Savannah, they would be lost for good.

What she'd planned would be dangerous for her and would hinge upon Howard Lee keeping the cellar door open when he came down to get the girls. He'd never closed it before and the plan would work only if he kept to the routine.

And she'd talked to the girls. Justine knew what to do and was excited to the point of hysteria, but Amy Anne had only listened. Mary wasn't certain if she even understood what was expected, but she had to be sure.

Taking both girls by the hand, she sat down on the bed and scooted them up on her lap.

"Justine, can you be a brave girl for me?"

"Oh, yes!" she said, her eyes sparkling with anticipation.

"When Howard Lee comes back, do you remember what to do?"

"We hide by the wall and don't make any sounds, and when he comes down, you yell for us to run and we go up the steps and out of the house."

"And what else?" Mary asked.

"We yell for help and we don't stop running or yelling until someone calls the police."

"Right," Mary said.

Justine wiggled with excitement, picking nervously at the buttons on Mary's shirt as she thought about getting home. Then a thought occurred and she started to frown.

"But what if he follows us? He's got very long legs. He'll catch us and then he'll be mad."

Mary hugged them close, making herself smile.

"No, no, remember what I said. He can't follow you because I'm going to grab him by the legs. I'll hold on very, very tight. He won't be able to move and you can get far, far away."

"Oh yes! I remember!" Justine said.

"Good," Mary said, then she looked at Amy Anne. She was so small and so quiet—a tiny doll with big blue eyes on the constant verge of tears. "Honey, do you understand what you need to do, too?"

Amy Anne was looking down at her shoes, not

talking, not moving. Mary put a finger under Amy Anne's chin and tilted her face until they were face to face.

"Amy Anne...do you want to go home?"

Tears welled in the her eyes as she stared at Mary's face. Finally, she nodded.

Mary cupped her face with both hands. "When I tell you to run, will you run with Justine? Will you run as fast as you can and never look back?"

Amy Anne nodded.

"Good girl. Okay, you girls go sit where I showed you to sit. I'm going to fix the beds so it looks like you are in them asleep. That way Howard Lee will see the lumps and think it's you. I'll make sure he comes toward me. As soon as he's far enough in the room, I'll shout for you to run. When I do, Justine, you grab Amy Anne by the hand and you girls run up the stairs and out of the house as fast as you can."

Justine quivered, she was so excited. "I will be home tonight, won't I, Mary?"

Mary hugged them tightly. "Yes, baby...you and Amy Anne will be in your very own homes tonight. You'll be with your mommies and daddies and this man won't ever hurt you again."

"And you, too," Justine said.

Mary's heart twisted. Her fate wasn't nearly as certain, but she wasn't going to tell the girls.

"Yes, darling, me, too."

"And we will come and play with Hope."

At the thought of her own little girl, her determination not to cry in front of them nearly splintered. Her voice was shaking as she gave them a last quick hug.

"Yes, baby...you'll both come and play with

Hope. Now go get in your places and remember, when you hear him opening the cellar door, don't talk...don't move.''

"Okay," Justine said, and took Amy Anne by the hand and led her toward the stairs.

Mary jumped up quickly and began padding the beds, making it appear as if the girls were under the covers asleep. Then she poured a glass of water in the middle of the floor a good distance away from the stairs, positioned herself to look as if she'd slipped in the water and fallen, then waited for Howard Lee.

Howard Lee tossed the last of his shirts into his suitcase, emptied the drawer containing his underwear and socks on top of them, and closed the lid. The rest of his clothes that were on hangers had been loaded in the van next to the pallets he'd made for the girls. He'd packed an ice chest with food and drink and packed his camping port-a-potty into the back of the van. Now all he needed was the girls and their clothes and he was ready to go. He glanced at his watch. It was just after 2:00 p.m. If he hurried, he'd be on the road and out of the city long before rush hour hit.

He reached into his pocket to get the key to unlock the cellar door, and then stopped and looked around for the rope. He didn't want Sophie. No, that was wrong. He had to stop thinking of her as that. Her name was Mary, and he couldn't afford to let her go.

The rope was on the floor near the door, right beside his hunting knife. He picked up the rope, stood for a moment looking down at the knife, then bent down and dropped it in his pocket.

His expression was grim as he unlocked the padlock on the cellar. All the way down the stairs he kept telling himself he could do this—that what he was planning wasn't a crime. A real father would do anything—even murder—to protect his family.

Then he saw her in the small pool of water—lying crumpled and still upon the floor. Her eyes were closed, her lips slightly parted, as if she'd been in the act of crying out when she'd slipped. He dropped the rope at his feet and ran toward her.

The empty glass was near her hand, the water still puddled beneath her body. He could only guess at what must have happened. He looked toward the beds and saw that the girls had gone back to sleep, which was good. It would make them easier to move to the van. But first, he needed to make sure Mary would not hinder his plans.

He bent down, reaching for her shoulders to drag her out of the way, when she suddenly came alive. Before he knew it, she had grabbed him by the ankles and yanked. He went down like a felled ox, thumping his head on the floor and momentarily knocking the wind from his body.

Mary crawled the length of his body, wrapped her arms around the upper part of his thighs, locked her legs below his knees, then held on. She held on for her life—and for Justine and Amy Anne.

"Run!" she screamed. "Run as fast as you can and don't look back!"

Both little girls bolted up from where they'd been crouching and ran up the steps, already screaming for help, just as Mary had told them.

A low groan came up and then out of Howard Lee's lips as he slowly came to. Almost immediately, he realized what she'd done and grabbed Mary by the hair, yanking viciously as he struggled to get free.

"You bitch! You bitch! You're ruining everything. Let me go!"

Mary ducked her head, shielding her face from his blows and tightened her grip.

Howard Lee struggled to sit up, but couldn't shake Mary's grasp. Then he heard the sound of little girls screaming and realized they were gone. Rage swamped him.

"What have you done? What have you done?" he screamed, then doubled up his fists and began raining blow after blow upon her shoulders and the back of her head as they rolled from side to side on the wet floor.

Mary cried out in pain, adding her own screams for help and prayed for a miracle.

"How far away from Raleigh Avenue?" Daniel asked.

"About three blocks. The house should be in the middle of the block on the left," Bobby Joe said, downshifted to pass a biker, then shifted back into high gear as soon as they were past him. "Think we should call Arnaud?"

"And tell him what? That we're looking for the man from a dream?"

"Yeah, right," Bobby Joe said and then suddenly braked when two little girls darted out from between some shrubbery and ran into the street.

"Son of a—"

He swerved sideways, bringing the car to a sliding halt only inches from the little girls' feet. Immediately, he and Daniel were out and running.

"Help! Help!" they screamed.

"It's okay, it's okay," Daniel said, and went down on his knees, gathering both girls in his arms. "You're all right. The car didn't hit you." Then he looked up and around, expecting to see a parent somewhere nearby.

"Where are your parents?" he asked.

"We don't know. The man took us. He wouldn't let us go home. Mary grabbed him and told us to run. She said to yell for help, so we ran and ran. You have to call the police before the man finds us again."

Daniel's heart skipped a beat as he took her by the arms and held her still.

"Who's Mary? Please, baby...who's Mary?" he asked.

Justine shivered. "The man brought her. She slept with us and she yelled at the man. She made him mad."

Daniel started to shake. "Honey...what's your name?"

"Justine." Then she tugged on the other girl's hand. "This is Amy Anne. Mary said we could go home."

"Sweet God," Daniel said, and then picked them up in his arms and ran toward the car, yelling at Bobby Joe as he went. "Call 9-1-1. Tell them we found the missing girls and tell them to contact Arnaud."

Bobby Joe yanked his phone from his pocket as Daniel slid into the seat, still holding both girls in his arms.

"Honey, are you okay? Did the man hurt you? Is Mary okay?"

"Do you know our Mary?" Justine asked.

It was all Daniel could do to answer without coming undone.

"Yes, honey, I know Mary. She's my Mary, too."

Justine smiled. "She wants to go home."

"Where is she, honey? Did the man keep you in his house?"

"Not exactly," Justine said.

"Then where. You have to tell me, honey, so I can go find her."

"Kind of like a basement, only nicer than the one at my house."

"Okay. That's a good girl. Mary will be proud of you."

Bobby Joe jumped into the car.

"The dispatcher patched me through to Arnaud. He's already on the way, and there was a cruiser only a couple of blocks from here. They'll be here any minute."

Daniel could hear the sounds of an approaching siren, but Mary had obviously put herself between the children and danger to make sure they escaped. He owed it to her to make sure they were safe.

"You stay with the girls," he said. "I'm going after Mary."

Bobby Joe frowned. "No way, man. Don't leave me alone with two kids."

Daniel set both the little girls in the seat beside Bobby Joe.

"They won't hurt you," he said. "Consider them little women in waiting, use your considerable charm on them until the police get here and you'll be fine."

"Damn it, Daniel, don't—"

Daniel was out of the car and running before

Bobby Joe could finish. The last thing he heard was one of them telling Bobby Joe that he shouldn't say bad words. If he hadn't been so scared, he would have laughed.

Howard Lee couldn't believe what was happening. He'd beaten this woman almost senseless and she still wouldn't let go. With unfettered rage, he thrust his hands into her hair and pulled, yanking her head backward and baring the tender underside of her throat. At that moment, he remembered his knife.

"I'll show you," he shrieked. "You'll be sorry you came between me and my girls."

He turned loose of her hair and began trying to get his hands in his pockets, while Mary struggled to stay conscious.

Every bone in her body throbbed from the beating she was taking and her vision kept going in and out of focus. She was so tired and too weak to hold on much longer, but letting go meant certain death. She heard him muttering and cursing and closed her ears to the sounds. She couldn't think about what he was doing to her. All she could do was hold on.

Daniel ran, his long legs marking off the distance between him and Mary Faith. He took shortcuts through lush, green lawns and down the alleys between houses, startling one lady who was in her backyard watering flowers and causing dogs in neighboring yards to start barking. The woman jumped back in fright, thinking she was about to be attacked. When Daniel ran past her instead, she dashed into her house and locked the door.

Daniel ran with Mary's name in his heart, remembering what Justine had said, that Mary grabbed the man by the legs and then told them to run. God. He'd never known she had that kind of strength. He needed to find her. He needed to find her alive—so that he could tell her how proud he was to call her his wife. He lengthened his stride, and moments later come out of an alley from between two houses to find himself in the middle of Raleigh Avenue. He paused briefly, his heart pounding and gasping for breath, uncertain of which way to go. The houses in front of him had no house numbers and the one behind him was missing two and the others were so faded he couldn't read them.

He turned in place, trying to find a numbered house on which to fix his location, and as he did, saw an elderly man coming toward him on the sidewalk with a small dog on a leash.

"Which way to 1449 Raleigh?" he yelled.

The man pointed over his shoulder.

Daniel bolted past him, praying for strength as he ran.

Halfway down the block, he began hearing the faint, but persistent, shriek of sirens. Although help was on the way, it didn't slow his steps. Moments later, he saw the numbers he'd been looking for, then the front door standing ajar at the house. He remembered the panicked looks on those little girls' faces, imagining their terror as they made their escape. In two long steps, he cleared the curb and was running through the yard.

Even before he was inside, he heard them fighting. Male rage mingling with a woman's weak, high-pitched shrieks sent a rush of adrenaline through his body. He hit the porch on the run, shouting Mary's name as he went.

Howard Lee's shirt was stuck to his body. His straight, Dutch-boy haircut was wet with sweat as he struggled to get the hunting knife out of his pocket.

"Move, bitch, move," he screamed, and whacked at Mary's shoulder with his fist. He felt her flinch, but she wouldn't let go and he couldn't get his hand in his pocket.

Mary continued to fight, screaming when she could gather the breath. A few seconds ago she'd thought she'd heard Daniel's voice and knew that was impossible. Daniel didn't know where she was. Maybe she was dying.

Suddenly, Howard Lee bucked and she went flying across the floor before hitting the wall in a sliding thump. Instantly, she rolled to her hands and knees as Howard Lee was pulling the knife from his pocket. She struggled to her feet and looked around for a weapon, but there was nothing. When he started toward her, she began backing up, using her hands for a shield as Howard Lee slide the blade from its sheath.

The sight of the weapon splintered her courage.

"Oh God…no, please no," Mary begged, and reached behind her, her fingernails raking the concrete surface of the walls as she faced her mortality.

"You destroyed my family!" Howard Lee shrieked.

Mary couldn't believe what she was hearing. He was going to kill her and then blame her for her own death? Not while she had breath in her body. She yanked the spread from one of the beds and wrapped it around her arm as he came at her.

"You're crazy! You don't have daughters. You stole someone else's. I'm not your wife! I belong to—"

"Mary! Mary!"

Mary gasped. That was Daniel! She hadn't imagined it before. She could hear him calling her name.

"Here!" she screamed. "I'm down here!"

Before Howard Lee could turn around, Daniel hit him from behind in a tackle worthy of the NFL. Howard Lee grunted. The knife went flying out of his hands. Once again, he went down, this time reaching outward and bracing himself for the fall. As he hit, his neck popped and he bit his own tongue. The coppery taste of blood spurted inside his mouth as he struggled to right himself beneath the weight of the man's body, but it was no use. Instead, he covered his head with his hands and started begging for mercy.

Reese Arnaud and Bobby Joe Killian came to a sliding halt in front of the house on Raleigh Street at almost the same time. They both came out of their cars, armed and running.

"Look for a basement," Bobby Joe yelled, as he vaulted onto the porch. "The kid said he kept them in a basement."

They entered the living room, one only a half step behind the other and then followed the sounds of the high-pitched screams into the bedroom, then down the cellar steps.

Reese was the first to reach bottom.

"Get Mary out of here," he yelled, and stepped

aside as Bobby Joe dashed past. Then he holstered his gun and moved toward Daniel. He needed to pull him off the man before he killed him.

"Daniel! Daniel…let him go!"

But Daniel didn't relent, which left Reese with the job of making it happen. He wrapped his arms around Daniel's upper body and pulled, wrenching the beaten and bloody man out of Daniel's grasp and leaving him limp and moaning on the floor.

Daniel spun, his fists still doubled, at the ready to throw another punch when he realized it was Reese.

"Son of a bitch," he muttered, and then took a deep, shuddering breath.

"Leave enough for me to arrest, and go tend to your wife."

Mary! Daniel spun, his gaze wide and frantic. Then he saw her slumped over on the bed. Bobby Joe stood between them, his gun still drawn. Daniel's legs were shaking as he took the first step. Was she all right? Had he come too late?

"Ah God…Mary."

She staggered to her feet and into his arms.

The moment Daniel's arms went around her, Mary started to cry—huge, choking sobs that ripped up her throat and burned the back of her nostrils. She threw her arms around his neck and pressed herself fast to his strength, praying that this wasn't another horrible dream and that he was really, truly here.

"The girls…the girls…did you find them? Are they okay?"

"Yes, baby…the girls are fine. We found them a few minutes ago."

"Thank God," Mary muttered, then felt the world going black.

Daniel caught her as she fainted, then swept her up in his arms. He looked down at Howard Lee, his rage still intact.

"Consider yourself lucky, you miserable son of a bitch. I would have killed you for what you did."

With Reese Arnaud already in the act of hand-cuffing the man, he sidestepped what was left of Howard Lee and carried Mary up and out of the basement, knowing Bobby Joe was right behind him. Sunlight hit him full in the face as he walked out of the house. He looked down at Mary, wincing at the array of bruising that he could see, and started to cry.

"There's an ambulance on the way," Bobby Joe said.

"I won't let her go."

Bobby Joe put a hand on Daniel's shoulder.

"That's all right, buddy. You don't have to. You'll be with her all the way."

Mary woke up in the ambulance and began to struggle.

"Let me go. Let me go," she mumbled. "Got to find the girls."

Daniel leaned over and cupped her face. "Mary...honey...the girls are fine. You're on your way to the hospital and I'll be with you every step of the way."

"Can't close my eyes...don't close my eyes. He'll take them away."

"He can't touch you, baby. He'll never bother anyone again."

"Don't drink the juice. It will put you to sleep."

"God Almighty," Daniel said, and laid his face against her shoulder.

The paramedic put his hand on Daniel's shoulder. "Hey, mister, she's going to be okay."

Daniel nodded through tears. "Yes, I know, but I'm not so sure about myself."

Chapter 15

Mary woke up once in the night, panicked at the unfamiliar surroundings, then she saw Daniel slumped over in a chair beside her bed.

Is this real or am I dreaming?

"Daniel?"

He jerked. Seconds later he was on his feet and at her side.

"Baby...what's wrong? Are you in pain? Do you want me to get the nurse?"

"No. I just needed to touch you...to know if you were real."

Daniel took her hand and lifted it to his lips, pressing a kiss in the palm of her hand.

"I'm real, baby...and so are you." He drew a deep, shuddering breath. "God, Mary...I've never been so scared."

"Me, too."

Gently, he lifted the wayward strands of hair from her forehead, then bent down and kissed her.

"The girls...they told us what you did. I am so proud of you."

"Are they all right?"

"Yes...oh, and Reese said that Justine wanted you to know that Amy Anne talked. Is that important?"

Mary closed her eyes briefly, picturing the silent child with horror-filled eyes.

"Very important. She was the first one he took. She was alone with that...that man...for almost a month before he took Justine. By that time she wouldn't make eye contact or react in any manner to what was happening. All the time I was with them I kept thinking...what if this had happened to Hope?"

"You saved their lives, honey. You're a real heroine, did you know that?"

"Does the media know about me?"

"No. At my request, Reese kept it quiet...mostly because of Hope."

Mary sighed. "Thank God. Could we please keep it that way?"

"You can have anything you want," Daniel said.

She tried to smile and then winced from the pain in her jaw. "What I want is to turn over, but I think I'm going to need some help."

"Sure, honey," Daniel said, and slid his hands beneath her shoulders. Just as he started to lift, she cried out in pain. He withdrew immediately, uncertain as to how he had hurt her.

"Mary...darling, I'm so sorry. What did I do?"

She grabbed his hand. "No, Danny...I'm the one who's sorry. I didn't mean to frighten you. It's just that my back and shoulders are so sore."

"Your back? What did he do?"

"I had to stop him from running after the girls, so I grabbed his legs. The only way I could keep him from kicking me loose was to wrap myself around the lower half of his body. I had control of his mobility, but not his fists."

"He beat you?"

The tone in Daniel's voice was chilling. Mary knew he was struggling with a terrible rage. She tried to make light of it by teasing.

"I stuck to him like a tick. You should have heard him screaming at me to let go."

"The bastard," Daniel muttered. "Let me see."

He turned on the light and then opened the back of her gown. Her skin was a mass of bruises, ranging in color from faint blue to a deep, dark purple. Some of them bore deep scratches, as if he tried to claw himself free. The shock of what Mary had endured made him sick. He stroked her arm, then her face, then lowered his head until their foreheads were touching.

"Oh sweet heaven...oh baby...I didn't know. I didn't know."

"Daniel...don't. They will heal and I still want to turn to my side."

Still Daniel hesitated. Mary sighed. The shock on his face was impossible to miss.

"Please," she begged, and then gritted her teeth when Daniel slid his hands back beneath her body and began to help her turn.

Groaning softly from the relief, she settled into a new position.

"Thank you, darling. That's much better."

Daniel stared at her without moving.

"How is Hope? Is she with Mike and Phyllis?"

"Yes, and she's fine. She doesn't even know you were gone."

Mary sighed. "What's the date today?"

"The 2nd of October."

"Oh no…it's her birthday. What's she going to think?"

"She doesn't know what day it is. Mom and Dad made sure of that. We'll celebrate her birthday when we're all home together."

"That's good."

There was a brief and uncomfortable moment of silence. Neither Mary or Daniel could think of a safe topic of conversation.

"Do you need anything for pain?" Daniel finally asked.

"No," Mary said, and then to her horror, felt tears rolling down her face.

For Daniel, it was the proverbial last straw. Rage spilled out of him in violent waves, making his body tremble.

"I should have killed the son of a bitch."

"Just hold me," Mary begged.

He lowered the bed rail and crawled in beside her. Sliding his arm beneath her neck, he pillowed her head on his chest and held her while she cried. He wanted to tell her that whatever that man had done to her would never destroy what was between them. He wanted to say it—but he was afraid to bring it up and so he held her and thanked God that she was still alive.

Several minutes passed, then several more, and Daniel was certain that Mary had fallen asleep. He figured he would catch hell from the first nurse to come in and find him in bed with her, but he didn't really care. He closed his eyes, trying to make himself relax. One moment led to another and then another, and just when he was on the verge of going under, he heard Mary's voice. The words were slurred, as if she were talking in her sleep, but they were a gift, just the same.

"He didn't rape me."

Ah God...thank you for sparing her that. "It's okay, baby...go back to sleep," he said softly.

Mary sighed. Her breathing slowed and he felt her muscles relax.

"Daniel..."

"What, honey?"

"The baby is okay."

He smiled to himself. She was so sleepy she was barely making sense.

"Yes, honey...Hope is okay."

She sighed. "Not Hope. The baby." Then she reached for his hand and laid it on her stomach. "Our baby," she mumbled, and fell back to sleep.

Daniel went from shock to elation. He splayed his fingers across her belly and realized that she hadn't just been fighting for Justine and Amy Anne's lives, but for the life of her unborn child. He laid his face against the back of her neck, unashamed of the tears that he shed.

"Thank you, Mary Faith," he said softly.

And then it was morning.

Mary was going to be dismissed, but she had adamantly refused to wear her dirty clothes ever again, and at her insistence, Daniel had gone home to get her some clean clothes.

She had showered earlier, and was sitting on the side of the bed in her gown and robe, waiting for Daniel to come back when she heard a knock at the door.

"Come in," she called.

The door swung slowly inward, and then Mary started to smile. She didn't recognize the four adults, but she knew the two little girls with them. She slid off the bed and then opened her arms.

"My heroes," she cried, and gathered them close to her breast. "Did you girls know that you saved me?"

Justine nodded importantly, while Amy Anne ducked her head and then buried her face in the curve of Mary's neck. Mary looked up then, remembering the adults who'd come with them.

"Where are my manners?" she said. "Please sit down."

"Not until you get back in bed," one of the women said.

Justine took Mary by the hand. "We'll help you, won't we, Amy Anne?"

Amy Anne nodded, then looked nervously toward her parents.

"The girls can sit with me," Mary said, as she got back in bed, and helped both of them up in her lap.

Justine giggled as they snuggled close. "This is the way we slept in the room, isn't it, Mary?"

Mary's eyes filled with tears. "Yes, it sure is."

The parents gathered around her bed, all talking at once. Finally, it was Amy Anne's father, Michael Fountain, who spoke for them all.

"We don't know how to thank you," he said, his voice breaking with emotion. "Justine told us what you did. You saved their lives, and we will be forever in your debt.''

"No," Mary said. "You don't owe me anything." She thought back to the day she'd walked into that antique shop. "I didn't used to believe this, but I do now. I think everything happens for a reason. Even the bad stuff. We don't always understand why, but, eventually, it finally becomes clear. I was in that place because it was meant to be. I had to be there because of them, so don't thank me, thank God. He's the One who made it possible."

Then she hugged both the girls and tickled Amy Anne's ear.

"Do you remember what we promised we would do when we got to go home?"

To Mary's surprise, it was Amy Anne who answered.

"Play with Hope."

Mary laughed with delight, then began to explain to the parents.

"Hope is my little girl. Yesterday was her seventh birthday, but the party has been a little delayed. I kept telling the girls that they would soon see you again, and that when you said it was okay, that they could come and play with Hope."

"It's a promise," they echoed, then added, "And it's also time for us to go. You need to rest, but the girls were adamant about coming to visit. I think they needed to see for themselves that you were all right."

Mary hugged them close. "I am very okay, aren't I?"

Justine's mother handed Mary a card.

"Just a little something from all of us for what

you did. Our phone numbers and addresses are enclosed. Please stay in touch.''

''Thank you,'' Mary said, and kissed both of the girls goodbye. As she did, it made her think of Hope and how badly she needed to hold her own child again.

They left as quietly as they'd come. Mary waved until the door went shut, then she turned the card over, smiling to herself at the awkward writing of her name. Something told her that Justine and Amy Anne had done it themselves.

She slid a fingernail beneath the flap and popped it open, then pulled out the card. As she read the verses, the hair on the back of her neck began to crawl.

A promise made is a thing to behold
A promise kept is worth more than gold.
So I promise you forever a love strong and true
Because you kept your promise when I needed you.

Justine and Amy Anne had signed it, one in green pencil, one with a pink marker. But it was the verse that gave her a chill. She closed her eyes, picturing the antique store and the sign, Time After Time. She saw herself going inside, then moving down the narrow, dusty aisles to the back of the store—finding the jewelry case and then that ring. That marvelous ring that had let her change the future and her fate.

There had been an engraving inside.

I promise you forever.

Forever was a long, long time with Daniel at her side.

She leaned back against the pillows as the last of her uncertainty ebbed. As she waited for him to come back, she felt a tiny flutter beneath her heartbeat. A sigh of contentment slid through her, filling her with such a sense of peace.

Yes, baby...I know you're still there.

Then she laid her hand on the flat of her stomach, as if in comfort to the tiny spark of new life that still burned.

The girls weren't the only ones who were depending on me, were they, sweet thing?

She closed her eyes, letting the silence envelope her. A few minutes later, she heard the familiar tread of Daniel's footsteps and sat up on the side of the bed, awaiting him with a smile.

Epilogue

The staircase at the O'Rourke house was entwined with fresh pine boughs and holly, and in the living room, the lights twinkled brightly on the six-foot Norfolk pine that Daniel, Mary and Hope had decorated last night. The scents of fresh greenery mingled with a simmering potpourri of sweet spices that Mary had going on the sideboard. She sat cross-legged in the floor in front of the tree, staring up at the lights, wanting to be close to the joy. Then her gaze slid to a very obviously handmade elf hanging from the lower branches.

Last night she'd watched Hope pull it from the box of decorations and listened to her chatter as she reminisced about making it at school the year before. It had been made from a juice carton and a dozen or so multicolored pompons. It looked more like an explosion of fuzzy M&M's, than one of Santa's elves. The odd thing was, Mary thought she could remember watching Hope hang it proudly on the tree, when she knew in her heart she'd been very alone last year. The transition between her life before the antique shop and her life after was something she would never be able to share, but however it happened, she was forever thankful.

Her wounds from the abduction had long since healed, although there were still nights when she woke up in a sweaty panic, thinking she was still fighting Howard Lee Martin for her life.

Both Justine and Amy Anne were still in therapy but had become fast friends with Hope. With the naïveté of the child that she was, Hope had blithely accepted them as Mommy's friends who had now becomes hers, as well.

Howard Lee Martin had never gone to trial, but Daniel had assured Mary that the institution for the criminally insane where he had been committed was a far worse sentence than anything else he could have ever received. He would never see the light of day as a free man again, and for Mary and the little girls' families, it would have to suffice.

Her life was peaceful and filled with joy on a daily basis. She went to bed each night with a prayer of thanksgiving on her lips and woke up each morning, grateful for what she had. By this time next year, there would also be an addition to their family and for that Mary was ecstatic. She'd missed all those early memories with Hope, but she wasn't going to miss them again.

She glanced at the clock. It wasn't quite ten. She still had time to run a quick errand before she met Daniel for lunch and she didn't want to be late. Even though she was moving on with her new life, there

was a part of her old one she needed to put to rest.
She got to her feet, grabbed her coat and her purse
as she headed out the door.

The December wind was chilly, even for Savannah, and Mary was glad that she'd worn her long
coat. She had been walking for blocks, trying to re-
trace the steps that she'd taken on the day her life
had changed. Yesterday she'd taken a chance and
called the dress shop where she once had worked,
only no one there even knew her name. She accepted
it as part of the confirmation for which she was
searching, but she still wanted to see the old man.

She'd found the Mimosa easily, the restaurant
where she'd been supposed to meet her friend. From
there, she'd walked up and down the renovated area
of the old town, admiring the Christmas decorations
in the windows while trying to find the antique store.
But each time she turned down a new block, she
came up empty. Frustrated, she thought about calling
Daniel for directions, then discarded the notion. It
would do nothing but worry him if he thought she
was still locked in the past.

She glanced at her watch and then sighed. If she
didn't start back to the parking garage where she'd
left her car, she would be late meeting Daniel for
lunch.

She started to turn away when she noticed the window display in the jewelry store next door. Something about it rang a bell. She moved closer to look
inside and realized she'd been here before.

She turned abruptly, expecting to see the antique
store directly across the street, but there was nothing
but an empty lot. She frowned, thinking maybe she

was confused about the area, then saw the knitting shop that had been on the east side of Time After Time. It was still there, as was the small coffee shop on the west, only there was nothing in between the two small businesses but dirt lot and space. Curious as to what had happened in the months since she'd been here, she hurried across the street to inquire.

The knitting shop was small; overflowing with a bounty of yarns—opulent mohair, baby-soft cottons, as well as the sturdy, multi-hued wools. But Mary's interest was not on the well-stocked store. She wanted to know what had happened to the shop that had been next door.

"Good morning," the clerk said, as Mary walked up to the counter. "May I help you find some yarns?"

"Actually, I need some information about the store that was next door."

"You mean the coffee shop?"

"No, the antique store."

The clerk frowned. "I'm sorry, ma'am, but there's no antique store in the area."

Mary looked at the woman as if she'd suddenly lost her mind.

"It was here in September and so was I. How long have you worked here?"

"Ever since my mother retired, which is almost ten years now."

Mary's palms started to sweat. This wasn't making sense.

"I don't understand. I was in the store only a couple of months ago. I talked to the old man behind the counter. There was dust all over the stock, but I was there."

"You must have the wrong street," the clerk said. "A lot of these blocks look alike, especially in the older part of the city."

"No. It was here," Mary said. "I distinctly remember standing across the street and seeing the reflection in that window." She pointed at the jewelry store across the street.

"I don't know what to tell you," the clerk said.

Before Mary could answer, the door to the back of the shop opened and a small, gray-haired woman came in.

"That's my mother. She's lived here all her life. Maybe she can help."

Mary nodded, although she couldn't imagine what the old woman might say that would eliminate this confusion.

"Mother, this lady is looking for an antique store. She thought—"

Mary interrupted. "It was on the lot between this store and the coffee shop. I was in there in September."

The old woman frowned. "No, honey…you must be mistaken. There hasn't been anything on that lot since the late twenties."

"But I was there," Mary said. "The store was called Time After Time and was full of dusty antiques."

"Not next door, you weren't," she said. "When I was a young girl, a man named Saul Blumenthal had a second-hand furniture store next door. He lived above it with his wife and baby boy. The store caught fire one night when Saul was at a meeting. By the time he got back, his business was gone and his family with it. It was the tragedy of our times."

''No,'' Mary muttered, remembering the sad eyes in the old man's face. ''That's not possible.''

The old woman shrugged. ''Well…it happened just the same.''

''What happened to Saul Blumenthal?'' Mary asked.

''Oh, that was the saddest part. A couple of days later, he hanged himself from what was left of the structure. I think they shipped the bodies back East to be buried.''

Mary took a deep breath and then walked out of the store. She paused on the sidewalk and then looked back at the lot, trying to make sense of what she'd just heard.

She hadn't dreamed it, because Daniel had mentioned the store more than once since she'd come home, commenting on the fact that when she'd passed out in the antique store it must have been because she'd been pregnant. Only she knew that hadn't been so.

As she stared at the small patch of dirt, she felt something against her face, like the breath of someone who'd passed too close to where she was standing.

But there was no one there.

Goose bumps rose on her arms as she shivered. She had no explanation for what had happened, but the longer she stood there, the more confused she became. There were all kinds of fancy words that some might apply to her story, should they have chosen to believe it.

Time travel.

Time warp.

By whatever name, it was still a mystery. Whether

it came from God's hand or an old man's wandering soul seeking forgiveness for what he had done by giving others a second chance, she knew what had happened. She didn't understand it. But she knew it was true.

She glanced at the empty lot one last time and then turned away, suddenly needing to be as far away from this place as she could get.

By the time she got to the parking garage, she was almost running. She slid behind the wheel and then took a deep breath. As she glanced at herself in the rearview mirror, she suddenly wondered why she'd been in such a hurry. She started the car and carefully backed out of the parking space. She still had a good half hour before it was time to meet Daniel. Taking a deep breath, she brushed the hair away from her face and accelerated carefully through the maze of ramps.

By the time she pulled out onto the street and headed downtown, the memories of her years without Daniel and Hope were swiftly fading and her mind was filling with all the things she needed to do before Hope's Christmas party at school.

She stopped at a red light and glanced at her watch. Someone honked loudly as they sped through the intersection. Startled by the sound, she looked up, and as she did, realized she didn't know where she was. Frowning, she glanced up at a street sign, trying to figure out why she was here and then shrugged. She must have taken a wrong turn on her way to meet Daniel for lunch.

The light changed and she drove through the intersection with a smile on her face. The further she drove, the fainter the past became. A few minutes later, she pulled up outside Daniel's office. When she saw him coming toward her with a smile on his face, what had been was no more. There was nothing left of who she'd been.

All she knew was right now, she was the luckiest woman on God's earth.

* * * * *

If you enjoyed what you just read,
then we've got an offer you can't resist!

Take 2 bestselling love stories FREE!
Plus get a FREE surprise gift!

**Where royalty and romance
go hand in hand...**

The series finishes in

with these unforgettable love stories:

THE ROYAL TREATMENT
by Maureen Child
October 2002 (SD #1468)

TAMING THE PRINCE
by Elizabeth Bevarly
November 2002 (SD #1474)

ROYALLY PREGNANT
by Barbara McCauley
December 2002 (SD #1480)

Available at your favorite retail outlet.

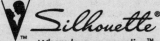

Where love comes alive™

COMING NEXT MONTH

#1177 THE PRINCESS'S BODYGUARD—Beverly Barton
The Protectors

Rather than be forced to marry, Princess Adele of Orlantha ran away, determined to prove that her betrothed was a traitor. With her life in danger, she sought the help of Matt O'Brien, the security specialist sent to bring her home. To save her country, Adele proposed a marriage of convenience to Matt—fueled by a very inconvenient attraction….

#1178 SARAH'S KNIGHT—Mary McBride
Romancing the Crown

Sir Dominic Chiara, M.D., couldn't cure his only son, Leo. Without explanation, Leo quit speaking, and child psychologist Sarah Hunter was called to help. Dominic couldn't keep from falling for the spirited beauty, as together they found the root of Leo's problem and learned that he held the key to a royal murder—and their romance.

#1179 CROSSING THE LINE—Candace Irvin

When their chopper went down behind enemy lines, U.S. Army pilot Eve Paris and Special Forces captain Rick Bishop worked together to escape. Their attraction was intense, but back home, their relationship crashed. Then, to save her career, Eve and Rick had to return to the crash site, but would they be able to salvage their love?

#1180 ALL A MAN CAN DO—Virginia Kantra
Trouble in Eden

Straitlaced detective Jarek Denko gave up the rough Chicago streets to be a small-town police chief and make a home for his daughter. Falling for wild reporter Tess DeLucca wasn't part of the plan. But the attraction was immediate—and then a criminal made Tess his next target. Now she and Jarek needed each other more than ever….

#1181 THE COP NEXT DOOR—Jenna Mills

After her father's death, Victoria Blake learned he had changed their identities and fled their original home. Seeking the truth, she traveled to steamy Bon Terre, Louisiana. What she found was sexy sheriff Ian Montague. Victoria wasn't sure what she feared most: losing her life to her father's enemies, or losing her heart to the secretive sheriff.

#1182 HER GALAHAD—Melissa James

When Tessa Earldon married David Oliveri, the love of her life, she knew her family disapproved, but she never imagined they would falsify charges to have him imprisoned. After years of forced separation, Tessa found David again. But before they could start their new life, they had to clear David's name and find the baby they thought they had lost.

SIMCNM0902